[*spectrum 6*]

For information on limited edition fine art prints by James Gurney
and Scott Gustafson call The Greenwich Workshop at 1-800-243-4246.

Trade Softcover Edition ISBN 1-887424-47-4
Hardcover Edition ISBN 1-887424-46-6
10 9 8 7 6 5 4 3 2 1

Special thanks to Phil Hale, Joe DeVito, Rick Berry, and Bud Plant
for always being willing to climb into the trenches.

This edition of Spectrum is gratefully dedicated to
TERRY LEE
who has always been there to take the desperate phone call for help.

Published by UNDERWOOD BOOKS, P.O. BOX 1609, GRASS VALLEY, CA 95945
www.underwoodbooks.com
TIM UNDERWOOD / *Publisher*

SPECTRUM 6
The Best In Contemporary Fantastic Art

edited by

Cathy Fenner & Arnie Fenner

UNDERWOOD BOOKS
GRASS VALLEY, CA 1999

chairmen's MESSAGE

by Cathy Fenner
and
Arnie Fenner

co-chairmen

d i r e c t o r s

Cathy Fenner
Arnie Fenner

advisory board

Rick Berry
Leo & Diane Dillon
Harlan Ellison
Bud Plant
Tim Underwood
Michael Whelan

elcome to the sixth annual celebration of the best in contemporary fantastic art. Similar in structure to other art competitions and annuals, *Spectrum* is unique in its focus and selection process. Featuring works that are characterized by their embracing of the themes of science fiction, fantasy, horror and the surreal, the contents of each book have been selected by a jury of peers through a strictly democratic process. One juror=one anonymous vote. With a simple plurality of votes a work of art is placed in the annual: no impassioned arguments, arm-twisting, or political considerations enter into the equation. At the end of the process, works receiving the most votes in each category are gathered: those with a simple majority are presented gold or silver awards. In the event of a tie, one or both chairmen and/or a member of the advisory board cast decision votes for award recipients. This process is constantly evolving and future modifications are inevitable.

The *Spectrum* competitions and subsequent annuals were started out of a frustration that the talents of many gifted creators were seemingly being overlooked and under-appreciated by both the illustration and the fine art communities for no other reason than their chosen subject matter. Believing that fantastic art, in all its myriad forms, is a worthy expression of intellect, skill, and imagination, the annual collections are the result of the conviction that there needed to be a record of *what* was being produced each year, *who* was doing it, and *where* the work was appearing.

Admittedly we don't have a precise definition of what constitutes "fantastic art" nor do we place constraints on the entrants regarding content or subject matter. Art is never selected strictly because it adheres to the trappings of genre, just as it's never rejected for being only very subtly "fantastic." If one annual features a gaggle of dragons while the next includes none, it is a reflection either of the quality and quantity of said entries in a given year or of the taste of the jury or both. Likewise the inclusion of nudes—the questioning of which is perplexing, given several thousand years of art history—is not done to make a statement or to arouse prurient thoughts, but solely because...it *is* art. *Spectrum* doesn't limit the creative muse by medium, morality or sensibility: to exclude work out of hand because it doesn't fit one taste or one definition of "fantastic art" would be no different than telling writers that they can only use certain words combined in a particular style to tell their stories.

Some have wondered why we didn't take an approach similar to the fiction "best of the year" compilations and simply select works of merit ourselves without going through the arduous procedure (and logistical challenge) of a Call For Entries and judging event. The most direct response is: No one can see it all and no *one*'s artistic taste is sacrosanct.

By reaching out to the artistic community through a blanket Call For Entries we can include pieces created outside of expected venues, works that are as yet unpublished, and art from other countries. By utilizing a diverse rotating jury for selection we insure that no *single* perception of "what's good and what isn't" dominates the contents year after year. The process requires the active participation of the artists or their representatives and their willingness to allow their work to be juried by their peers. It is a courageous act for a creator to essentially hold out their art—an investment of themselves—and ask, "What do you think?"

All of which is a way of explaining that this book, this series of books, exists because of the artists and their belief in the value of an annual forum. Not only the belief of those selected for inclusion within these pages, but of all whom have participated in the process, whom have supported this record of the fantastic arts. To them, to the jury, and to you the reader, we extend our collective thanks for continuing to make this series possible.   †

4 [*spectrum*]

STEVE MARK
Design Group Manager/Hallmark Cards

PHIL REYNOLDS
Art Director/Andrews McMeel

SUSAN SIFERS
Artist

JOHN JUDE PALENCAR
Artist

GEORGE DIGGS
Artist

KEN WESTPHAL
Artist

BUD PLANT
Illustration Historian

PHIL HALE
Artist

John BERKEY

"I knew exactly what I wanted to do from about the age of fifteen, and that was an advantage," John Berkey observes. "There was never a question whether I was wasting my time, it was always a direct shot to painting." Born in 1932 in Edgley, North Dakota, Berkey's clarity of purpose led him to summer jobs working for a variety of ad agencies and art studios throughout his high school years. As an "apprentice" he fetched a lot of coffee, emptied a lot of waste baskets, and provided paste-up for a lot of flyers and ad slicks. But he also learned a tremendous amount, not only about color and composition and painting, but also about what it means to be a commercial artist with fine arts sensibilities.

In 1955 John joined the staff of Brown and Bigelow in St. Paul, Minnesota. B&B at the time was the world's largest calendar company; art was either created by the 150 salaried illustrators or was purchased from some of the most prominent freelance illustrators of the day, including Norman Rockwell and Maxfield Parrish. Over the next eight years Berkey created something like 500 paintings covering a wide range of subjects, from landscapes to complex historic tableaus. Preferring to work and research at home rather than in a bustling office, John left B&B in 1963 to pursue freelance opportunities and has never looked back. His robust, contemporary-impressionist style immediately propelled him into the front ranks of America's illustrators and he was kept active painting book covers, advertisements, movie posters, and magazine illustrations for the likes of *The National Geographic*, *Life*, *Time*, and *TV Guide*.

Aficionados of fantastic art know John Berkey for his numerous science fiction book covers (including a painting for an obscure novelization of the screenplay for something called *Star Wars*). There is a type of majesty to his canvases; his cityscape spacecraft have a certain dignity, almost a sense of nobility, not unlike (and perhaps purposely) the sailing vessels of a lost age. There is the believable illusion of size and weight and speed of his ships despite their being rendered in bold, painterly brush strokes. His works are contradictorily detailed and minimalist. "To me, " John explains, "reality is *this is* while imagination is *what if?* A good space painting contains both *this is* and *what if*. In my early work, imagination was the energy that was contained within my drawings and paintings. Now imagination comes before and flows throughout the painting process. Imagination doesn't seem constant like sight, whether it be a thought or a mental picture, it is still presented as the question, *What if?*"

The purity of John Berkey's vision is obvious upon viewing the body of his work: *it does not age*. Each painting is as fresh and vibrant and far-thinking as the day it was created, whether that day was thirty years ago or just last Tuesday. That timeless quality is what sets him apart from the pack, that originality which insures that his work remains relevant: the qualities that make John Berkey a Grand Master. †

Y
ear

O

I
n

8

9

R
eview

b   *y*

S   *p*   *e*   *c*   *t*   *r*   *u*   *m*

A   *r*   *i*

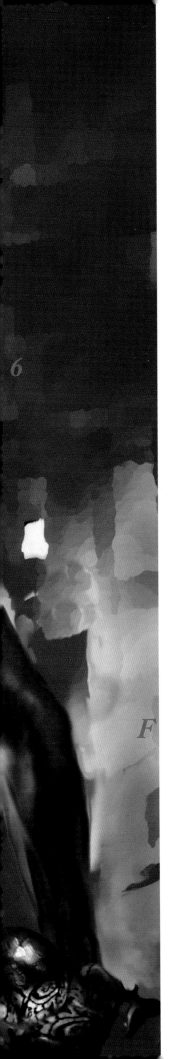

*E*lation. Confusion. Determination. Disappointment. 1998 found the world of fantastic art either an encouraging and exciting field of endeavor or a heartbreaking exercise in frustration. The same year that celebrated the induction of Grand Master Frank Frazetta into the prestigious Society of Illustrators Hall of Fame (only the third time in the Society's history that a "sci-fi" artist has been so honored) also found the legendary painter's copyrights blatantly infringed upon by the French publisher Éditions Cortelon with a bootleg book cobbled together from a variety of printed sources. The same year in which the comic book industry breathed a tentative sigh of relief (in hopes of a market revival) as Marvel shakily emerged from bankruptcy also witnessed the heretofore indestructible and creator-friendly Kitchen Sink Press close its doors once and for all. '98 was the year in which Internet sales of books sharply increased (along with online fraud) at the same time a host of web magazines floundered and, like *Omni Online*, died; it was the year in which creators contested various publishers' attempts to remarket their work on c.d.s without additional compensation; the year that saw the reshuffling of studio alliances and ties along with corporate mergers which conceivably threatened both the creative and small business communities alike; twelve months that saw anticipation for the new *Star Wars™* film build to a fever pitch as even the 6:00 News ran the coming attractions—uninterrupted!—as *news* stories; the year in which we were introduced to some remarkable new talents and said goodbye to legendary artists and friends. It was a year of transition—as I suppose every year is, in some form or another. So whatever one might say about 1998, it definitely couldn't be described as "boring."

ADVERTISING

Remember my comments over the past few years that computer-generated graphics were dominating the advertising arena? Well, nothing's changed.

Photoshop, the most commonly used software, has enabled designers to pretty much do anything with a photograph or toned image that their hearts desire, achieving effects that were in the past only possible of attaining through the use of an illustrator or a talented (and expensive) photo retoucher. Now show-stopping effects are routinely obtained with the click of a mouse, the smearing of a few pixels, and the application of a couple of filters—not necessarily better, but definitely faster than traditional painting, with an infinite number of variations at your fingertips (provided you hadn't flattened your file).

And since advertising has traditionally been the (potentially) most lucrative arena of commer-

e   *n*   *n*   *e*   *r*

cial art, it is understandable that illustrators have either been denouncing the digital revolution or enrolling at the community college for some computer classes—or both. Realistically, no matter how sophisticated technology becomes, it will never replace traditional pen and paint and paper entirely: nothing still *feels* or forms a uniquely human bond between creator and client like original art. Whereas with digital images there's always that sneaking suspicion, whether unfounded or not, that the computer did more work than the artist—and clients respond with a much more cavalier attitude.

Now, there is *always* a tremendous amount of fantastic art in print and on TV, but since advertising is a frustratingly anonymous field it is always difficult for me to credit worthwhile accomplishments; trying to identify an illustrator's work by *style* usually leaves me with egg on my face. But I did note exceptional art by Anita Kunz, Jerry LoFaro, Ezra Tucker, Barry Jackson, Mark Fredrickson, C.F. Payne, Bill Mayer, Ralph Steadman, Tim Jessel, and E.C. alumni Jack Davis—oh, and Ashley Wood's tasty promos for various Image comics were especially nice.

opposite: *Painting by Jon Foster and Rick Berry for a film proposal by Neil Gaiman*

Ahh, but if you want to talk *influence* and visual pyrotechnics one needn't have looked any further than Industrial Light & Magic's TV commercials for First Union: blending *Blade Runner* with Dean Motter's

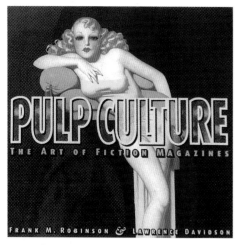

Robinson's and Davidson's Pulp Culture *joined '97's* Pulp Art *to form the definitive surveys of an almost forgotten segment of publishing history. Drawn from Frank's world-class collection,* Pulp Culture *featured an eye-popping assortment of classic images.*

stylish *Mr. X* comics, adding a dash of Dali and a pinch of Clive Barker's *Hellraiser*, ILM's city/hell tableau created a sensory feast that will surely be reinterpreted into a variety of other artists' paintings, films, and yes, more commercials in the years to come.

BOOKS

This really is an electrifying time in the book industry: that could be good or bad, depending on whether you're the one getting charged up or the guy getting his socks shocked off.

Profits were up (though the American Booksellers Association reported that three million fewer books were sold in 1998 when compared to '97); art fees were down. Stock images were less noticeable than last year, but graphic solutions for covers continued to battle narrative art for shelf dominance. A healthy number of fantastic-themed compilations were produced in 1998, but they were rarely treated as *art books* (how *presumptuous* to consider seem as such!) at the local superstore and were generally lumped in hodgepodge displays with gaming guides and graphic novels. (I *could* start my typical rant of how book artists have been increasingly treated as the bastard children of both the fantasy and science fiction community and the world of commercial illustration. About how the illustrators play

an indispensable role in creating a mass market for genre fiction through their arresting imagery and in return they've had to scrambled to make a living, usually in anonymity and...aaahh, don't get me started.) But probably the one story that had everyone within the industry talking was giant bookseller BarnesandNoble's announced plan to acquire equally giant book distributor Ingram. Concerns about the reliance of B&N's competitors on Ingram's services and worries about unfair trade advantages were loudly expressed on the business side (where independent retailers have already been adversely impacted by the large chains), while on the creative end alarm bells were sounded at the prospect of a major buyer having double the input on their art direction and offerings.

What's it all add up to? I won't even hazard a guess. Using simple logic one might draw some alarming conclusions, but the book industry is far from logical. Despite all the yadayada about electronic books, despite the rise of multinational, multimedia publishing corporations where marketing and accounting make all too many "creative" decisions with a cold eye staring at the financial bottom line, publishing, at it's core, is still an industry ruled by *passion*. As long as books are a product of love and conviction (regardless of the occasional buttheaded opinion), rather than a by-the-pound commodity, we can count on a continued wonderful selection of titles and art. Like we had in 1998.

Anyone who doesn't believe that this is a golden age for genre book art either isn't paying attention or is stuck in the '50s. I can think of no other time when such a diverse range of exceptional talents were simultaneously creating memorable works of fantastic art. Donato Giancola continued to stretch his artistic muscles with covers for *Deathstalker Honor* by Simon Green and *Queen of Demons* by David Drake [both published by Tor], as did Cliff Nielson with his exceptional paintings for *Dawn Song* by Michael Marano [Tor] and *The Crow: Lazarus Heart* by Poppy Z. Brite

1998 witnessed Frank Frazetta's induction into the Society of Illustrators Hall of fame and the release of his first major hardcover retrospective, Icon.

[Harper Prizm]. Michael Whelan returned to commercial work after a year of devoting himself to fine art with the cover to Tad Williams' *Otherland: River of Blue Fire* [Daw]; Kinuko Y Craft provided another classic vision for *Song of the Basilisk* by Patricia McKillip [Ace]; John Jude Palencar provided a glimpse of hell with his painting for *Tales of the Cthulhu Mythos* by H.P. Lovecraft [Del Rey]; and Dennis Nolan beautifully set the tone for *The One Armed Queen* by Jane Yolan [Tor]. Some of the many covers of note included works by Steve Crisp (*Lady Pain* by Rebecca Bradley [Gollancz]), Harry O. Morris (*Eyes of Prey* by Barry Hoffman [CD Productions]), Steve Hickman (*Dragon* by Steve Brust [Tor]), Ian Miller (*The Castle of the Winds* by Michael Scott Rohan [Orbit]), Rick Berry (*Bloom* by Wil McCarthy [DelRey]), Eric Dinyer (Connie Willis' *To Say Nothing of the Dog* [Bantam]), and Tom Canty (*Year's Best Fantasy and Horror* edited by Terri Windling and Ellen Datlow [St. Martin's Press]). Naturally, that's just the tip of the iceberg: excellent art was created by Romas, Don Maitz, Bruce Jensen, John Howe, Jim Burns, and Bob Eggleton, to name only a very few.

Gary Gianni's paintings and numerous drawings made *The Savage Tales of Solomon Kane* by Robert E. Howard [Wandering Star] the must-have illustrated edition of the year. Likewise, Phil Hale's brace of new canvases for a second edition of Stephen *King's Drawing of the Three* [Donald Grant] were reason enough to shell out for a reprint. On the other hand, the artists for *The Crow: Broken Lives & Shattered Dreams* anthology [Harper Collins] were poorly served by low production standards. Color works by Berry, Hale, Dan Brereton, Scott Hampton, Kent Williams, and eleven more were printed in muddy black and white. Though Donald Grant Books will be producing a collectors edition in color later in 1999, the projected $225 retail price insures that most will never see the art as it was intended. Other illustrated collections of merit included *The Cleft and Other Odd Tales* written and illustrated by

Gahan Wilson [Tor], the Dillon's celebratory *To Everything There Is a Season* [Blue Sky], Omar Rayyan's luscious *King Midas* [Holiday House], and Tolkien's *The Silmarillion* illustrated by Ted Nasmith [Harper Collins].

The year witnessed a welcome number of art books in various formats. *Heroes and Angels* [Archangel] was a beautiful compilation of Ray Lago's paintings. *Maximum Black* [Alderac Entertainment] was an edgy showcase for Tim Bradstreet while *Intron Depot 2: Blades* [Dark Horse] provided an equally arresting forum for *Ghost in the Shell* creator Masamune Shiro. Morpheus International released Wayne Barlowe's *Barlowe's Inferno*, *The Fantastic Art of [Zdzislaw] Beksinski*, and *Monsters From the Id: The H.R. Giger Bestiary* (which was originally created for the annual Sigraph computer conference). Another odd Giger item was *The Mystery of San Gottardo* [Taschen], supposedly a thirty year project published in journal form.

The Complete Etchings of Norman Lindsay [Odana], edited by Lin Bloomfield, was quite simply *the* book on the controversial Australian artist; *The World of Michael Parkes* provided a great survey of the art of "America's leading Magic Realist," and *The Art of Daniel Merriam: The Impetus of Dreams* was an exquisite compendium by one of the century's most respected surrealists. Cathy and I edited the appropriately titled *Icon*, the largest collection of work by Frank Frazetta yet assembled [Underwood Books], Dave Stevens' always stunning art was the subject of an over-sized poster book, *Vamps & Vixens* [Verotik], while *John Bolton: Haunted Shadows* [Halloween Concepts] reveled in it's erotic imagery of nude vampiresses. *Secret Mystic Rites: The Art of Todd Schorr* was an eye-popping excursion into weirdness, Simon Bisley's paintings for a projected animated film were collected in *F.A.K.K.²* [Heavy Metal], Luis Royo's powerful work was gathered in *III Millennium* [NBM], and Brian Froud returned to the popular fairy realm in *Good Faeries/Bad Faeries*, edited by Terri Windling [Simon & Schuster]. *Steve Stone: Nexus DNA* [Archangel] masterfully displayed a combination of both photography and computer abilities, Bob

Eggleton successfully experimented with a variety of techniques in *The Book of Sea Monsters* [Paper Tiger], Vanguard released the *Al Williamson Sketchbook*, and Harcourt Brace published Ralph Steadman's *Gonzo:*

Superman © & ™ 1999 DC Comics

Alex Ross' cover for Superman: The Complete Story, Les *Daniels' fun celebration of the Man of Steel for Chronicle Books.*

The Art. Kitchen Sink Press released the hardcover collection *Libertore's Women* and SQP continued with their line of b&w erotic books including *Sorceress* by Mike Hoffman, *Masquerade: The Art of Maren*, and the anthology titles featuring a variety of artists: *Eternal Temptation, Dragon Tails 2*, and *Crimson Embrace V*. All pretty innocent fun. But I'm not quite sure how to react to Hajime Sorayama's *Torquére* [Sakuhin-sha]: his enviable anatomy skills and expertise with an airbrush just can't compensate for the fact that this book is a collection of deeply disturbing images of beautiful women being tortured and mutilated. If there's a some sort of message (beyond, sadly, what seems obvious), it's getting lost in the translation.

Pulp Culture by Frank Robinson and Lawrence Davidson [Collectors Press] was a gorgeous tribute to the artists of a lost era; *Illustrators 39* [Watson-Guptill] included some fantastic imagery interspersed with the array of mainstream illustration; *Batman Masterpieces* [Watson-Guptill] compiled paintings by a number of artists (including Joe DeVito, Dave Dorman, Dermot Power, and Vincent

Difate) from the popular *Batman Master Series* trading cards; and *The Art of Mulan* [Hyperion] offered a tantalizing tour of the creative process behind the popular Disney film. A couple of fascinating books from 1998 further explored the imagery and icons of pop culture: *Batman: Animated* by Paul Dini and Chip Kidd [Harper Collins] examined all aspects of the stylish certainly-not-only-for-kids animated series while *Superman: The Complete History* by Les Daniels (also designed by Chip Kidd) [Chronicle] was a colorful 60th anniversary tribute to comics' most beloved character.

One would think that it should be easy to find most of these titles at your local bookstore or specialty shop. Unfortunately, distribution is often maddeningly spotty. So when I recommend Bud Plant Comic Art (P.O. Box 1689, Grass Valley, CA 95945—web catalog: www.budplant.com) each year as a single resource for art books of interest to *Spectrum* readers it's not because of our friendship: Bud Plant, simply put, has *the largest* selection of fantastic art product in stock than any other bookstore, traditional or virtual. Catalogs are available from the above address for $3.

COMICS

Depending on who you want to listen to, either the comic book market continues to shrink a little bit more each year or...the comic book market continues to shrink a little bit more each year. Over the past twelve months even many optimists started to see the symbolic glass as half empty. As toy "action figures" created exclusively for the specialty market began to dominate shelf space, retailers took fewer chances on diverse comic product—I could walk into any of the local comics shops on any given Wednesday and *not* find 1/10th of the comics, books, or magazines offered monthly through the distributor's catalog.

Plenty of action figures, though.

Marvel Comics finally had their re-organization plan approved by the bankruptcy courts and merged with Toy/Biz. But the once dominant company seemed panicky throughout 1998, curtailing their lines and engaging in some questionable actions against their free-lancers that was a public relations nightmare. Some additional unwanted publicity was generated when a typo (which unfortunately was an ethnic slur) slipped by the proofreaders of one of the *X-Men* titles: the subsequent recall of the comic only

Mike Mignola's Hellboy *continued to be thoughtful, frightening, and funny—and well-drawn to boot.*

caused more attention.

Industry watchers seemed genuinely surprised when Image co-creator Jim Lee sold his Wildstorm line to DC, but the demise of Kitchen Sink Press almost seemed expected. Lee and his Wildstorm creators and titles will continue to have a prominent place on the racks, but the fate of many of the edgier KSP titles that Denis Kitchen had championed remained unknown at year's end.

Diamond Comic Distributor sent a shiver down the industry's collective spine when it acquired the online retailer AnotherUniverse.com, Walmart rattled the publishers' cages by threatening to cease handling all of their titles because of the perceived adult content of a few, and creators went toe-to-toe with their clients over the translation of their works into other medias and mediums. Yow!

What about nice things? Sure, some nice things happened. The Hearst Foundation donated a million dollars to the Museum of Cartoon Art in Boca Raton, Florida; an auction at Sotheby's (with thanks to Jerry Weist) of original art from *Mad* realized a little over a million bucks;

the Comic Book Legal Defense Fund had only minor censorship cases to contend with during the year; and the professional community showed some heart as they contributed to benefit auctions for the wife of Charles Vess, Karen Shaffer, who had been injured in a car crash and was facing rehabilitation without health insurance.

So, yeah, despite some gloom and predictions of doom, there were some positive aspects to 1998. Including, of course, a batch of wonderful comic art.

DC might be considered (using a Cold War analogy) as the last remaining Super Power of the comic book industry. Certainly not immune to the vagaries of the marketplace, they were still sufficiently confident to experiment with formats, themes, characters, and contents. Superman once again received an appropriately mythic treatment in Alex Ross' *Peace* (written by Paul Dini) and in Tim Sale's mini-series *Superman For All Seasons* (written by Joseph Loeb); Bo and Scott Hampton played with the concept of alternate history with *Batman: Other Realms*, Dan Brereton's *Batman: Thrillkiller* (written by Howard Chaykin) was released as a trade paperback; and Glenn Fabry, Jim Murray, and Jason Brashill collaborated on *Batman/Judge Dredd: Die Laughing* (written by Alan Grant and John Wagner). Cajun magic was the theme of Ted McKeever's *Toxic Gumbo* (written by underground diva Lydia Lunch); Christopher Moeller beautifully tackled SF with his *Sheva's War* mini-series; and the manic *Batman/Hellboy/Starman* teamup by Mike Mignola (written by James Robinson) was rapid fire entertainment. Some of DC's noteworthy covers included those by Sean Phillips (*The Minx*), Michael Kaluta (*Witchcraft: La Terreur*), Glenn Fabry (*Preacher* and *Hellblazer*), Tony Harris (*Starman*), Doug Beekman (*Batman: Legends of the Dark Knight*), Jon J. Muth (*Swamp Thing: Roots*), the influential Dave McKean (*Essential Vertigo*) and various works by Jeffrey Jones, Glen Orbik, Brian Bolland, Herman Mejia, Joe Kubert, and Bruce Timm.

Dark Horse Comics spent a good percentage of '98 gearing up for 1999's premiere of *The Phantom Menace* with various additions to the *Star Wars* franchise (including some nice paintings by Ezra Tucker and Dave Dorman). Their *Alien* license also saw some new offerings, with David Wenzel's *Aliens: Stalkers* being one of the more interesting. *Godzilla* and *Starship Troopers* benefited from some excellent

covers by Bob Eggleton and Den Beauvais respectively. Though the film tie-ins are certainly what have helped keep Dark Horse financially viable during the industry's troubled times, it has always been their creator-owned titles that have especially shined artistically. Masakazu Katsura's *Shadow Lady: Dangerous Love*, Paul Chadwick's *Concrete: Strange Armor*, and Frank Miller's *300* were all carefully crafted, memorable comics. *Hellboy: The Chained Coffin & Others* by Mike Mignola was easily one of the year's best books: quirky, darkly funny, and beautifully drawn, Mignola's sporadic series was a reminder of the full possibilities of the medium. But Dark Horse's *real* page-turner of the year was a *book*, not a graphic novel. *Comics Between the Panels* by Steve Duin and Mike Richardson was an anecdotal behind-the-scenes encyclopedia of the comics field. Occasionally biased, sometimes insensitive, and often pretty damn funny, *Comics Between the Panels* proved fascinating for anyone remotely interested in the medium.

Sirius Entertainment, solidly anchored by various *Dawn* products beautifully rendered by Joseph Michael Linsner, published some stunning comics. Jill Thompson's *Scary Godmother: Holiday Spooktacular* and *Scary Godmother: The Revenge*, Mark Crilley's *Akiko*, Voltaire's *Chi-Chian*, and Dark One's *Animal Mystic: Water Wars* featured some of the most memorable art.

Image Comics, not yet smarting from the departure of the titles created by Wildstorm Productions, released a variety of interesting work. Todd McFarlane's *Spawn* continued to be the company's standard bearer, profitable both as a comic and as a licensable character. David Mack's *Kabuki* was stylistically appealing, Michael Gilbert's *Mr. Monster vs Gorzilla* was enjoyable, and Joe Chiodo's *The Mechanic* was impressive. Other Image creators that produced stand-out art included Alex Ross, Greg Capullo, Ashley Wood, J. Scott Campbell, Al Rio, Jim Lee, Travis Charest, and Adam Hughes.

Before Kitchen Sink was forced to close up shop it had released Dave McKean's moody and massive *Cages*. At nearly 500 pages, the book was a major event unfortunately overshadowed by the publisher's circumstances. Covers by Dave Gibbons, Mark Schultz, Brian Bolland, and William Stout were highlights of their abbreviated new *The Spirit* series.

Verotik showcased some exceptional art

by Kent Williams, Simon Bisley, and Milo Manara; Basement Comics included good work by Frank Cho, Bud Root, and Mike Hoffman; movie poster legend Drew Struzan turned up on the cover of *Astounding Space Thrills* #3; Jim Steranko proved that he had perhaps read one too many Mickey Spillane novels in his illustrated "biography" for *Tales From the Edge* #12 [Vanguard]; *Frank Frazetta Fantasy Illustrated* included stories by Daren Bader, Joe Jusko, and Tim and Greg Hildebrandt; and Bisley, Zook, and Manuel Sanjulian produced eye-catching covers for *Heavy Metal*.

Finally, I realize that I don't usually mention newspaper comic strips in the year-end review, partly because the local paper doesn't carry the most interesting titles and partly because I'm suffering from post *Calvin & Hobbes* depression. But I did want to point out two marvelous strips that are both well worth a look: Frank Cho's *Liberty Meadows* and Patrick McDonnell's extremely funny *Mutts*.

While the comics industry is sorely in need of an unbiased trade journal, there are several magazines that provide some insight into the field including *Comic Book Artist* (TwoMorrows, P.O. Box 204, West Kingston, RI 02892), *Comic Book Marketplace* (Gemstone, P.O. Box 180700, Coronado, CA 92178), and *The Comics Journal* (Fantagraphics, 7563 Lake City Way NE, Seattle, WA 98115).

DIMENSIONAL

After several years of meteoric growth the market for collectible statues, action figures, and model kits seems to have leveled out. The quantity and quality of pieces offered was still mind-spinning, but success was more hit and miss rather than a sure thing.

Tony McVey and his Menagerie Productions released a stunning four-foot-long T-Rex along with "Dinozilla," their refreshing and original take on the Japanese icon. Randy Bowen produced a batch of notable statues including "Dawn" based upon Joseph Michael Linsner's character, "Hellboy" (designed by Mike Mignola), "Solomon Kane" (inspired by Gary Gianni's version of the Robert E. Howard's creation), and a pair of original works: "Kongzilla" and "Bionica."

Alex Ross created the "Superman: Kingdom Come" macquette for DC; other DC characters like "Hellblazer" and "Green

SPECTRUM STUDENT COMPETITION

$1000 scholarship: JIN M. LIM
instructor: C.F. Payne   *school:* Columbus College of Art & Design

An experiment for this year's competition was a student category and the awarding of three small scholarships. The inclusion of a similar category in future *Spectrums* is being evaluated. In the meantime, we are proud to celebrate the work of these young artists of the next millennium

$500 scholarship: ERIC FORTUNE
instructor: Mr. Hazelrig
school: Columbus College of Art & Design

$300 scholarship: THOMAS L. HICKE II
instructor: Michelle Stutts
school: American Academy of Art

Lantern," were impressively handled by William Paquet. Dark Horse released cold-cast figures of *X-Files'* Mulder and Scully (sculpted by Carl Surges); Jaguar Models produced Susuma Sugita's sexy(!) alien, "Mother"; Barsom Manashim created "Auriel" for Mad House; and Mike James added "Agent Venus" [Azimuth Design] to his line of well-endowed fantasy pin-ups.

Moore Creations made it's presence known in all areas of the marketplace. Their version of David Mack's "Kabuki" (sculpted by the talented Schiflett Brothers) was a knock-out, while Clayburn Moore's various action figures were amazing. In fact, the only competition Moore has for quality in that particular arena is McFarlane Toys, which likes to market their figures as "conversation starters." Their *X-Files* movie tie-ins and various *Spawn* incarnations remained popular throughout the year.

There are several worthwhile magazines that cover the collectible model/figure market (*Amazing Figure Modeler* and *Kitbuilders* are only two), but if you surf the web a pair of great sites are Gremlins in the Garage (www.gremlins.com) and the Doll & Hobby Shoppe (www.doll-hobby.com).

EDITORIAL

So. Have you subscribed to your favorite virtual magazine yet? Me neither. And it's not because I'm a technophobe: I use computers everyday. But there is nothing more tedious than reading blocks of copy off a screen. I need the tactile feel of paper, the smell of fresh ink, the sound of a flipping page. A magazine has a *personality*, a true sense of *reality*: it relies on a disparate team of people—designers, editors, writers, accountants, marketing staff, typesetters, printers—all pulling together to achieve a common goal. It is the product of a *community* effort. Despite some razzle-dazzle, a website is something more to be looked *at* rather than *read*. (Which is why I like to visit a lot of artist's pages on the Internet.) Will that change? We'll just have to wait and see.

In the meantime, there was a welcome selection of good-old-fashioned ink-on-paper magazines on the racks during the year. A pleasant surprise was Wizards of the Coast's revived *Amazing Stories*. Art directed by Shauna Wolf Narciso, the field's oldest surviving publication (with a many-storied history) rapidly became one of its most artistically sophisticated titles with art by Anita Kunz, John Jude Palencar, Gary Kelley, and many more notables. Sovereign Media's *Science Fiction Age* and *Realms of Fantasy* included some exceptional work by John Berkey and Barclay Shaw in the former and profiles of Brian Froud, Brom, and Doug Beekman in the latter. Horror aficionados could look to *Cemetery Dance* for a cover by Phil Parks while the Goth crowd turned to *Carpé Nocturna* for a tasteful painting by Jon J. Muth.

The fiction digests, battling for space on the racks with their larger, more colorful competition, nevertheless seemed to hold onto their slice of the genre pie in 1998.

The Magazine of Fantasy and Science Fiction sported some effective covers by Jill Bauman, Ron Walotsky, and Kent Bash; *Analog* boasted some nice pieces by George Krauter and Jim Burns; and *Isaac Asimov's Science Fiction Magazine* included some attractive work by Burns, John Foster, and Bob Eggleton.

As always, fantastic art has never been limited to the genre fiction magazines nor to the cadre of illustrators that specialize in the field. That's one of the great things about fantastic art: it's everywhere. The

Talk about cool! This Necronomicon *volume was originally created by French artist Jean-Marc Laroche as the guest book for the Brussells Festival of Fantasy & Science Fiction Films. A 12-copy limited edition was available for $1500.00.*

offbeat film magazine *Outré* ran a great multi-part biography of comics legend Wallace Wood, along with articles on Vincent DiFate and Chesley Bonestell; the *New Yorker* included some wonderful graphic work by Art Spiegelman; and, of course, *Playboy* printed astonishing art by Gary Kelley, Donato Giancola, Phil Hale, and Rafael Olblinski, to name a mere handful. Magazines like *Communication Arts*, *Print*, *Graphis*, and *Step-By-Step Graphics* provided invaluable insights into current trends of the illustration world.

Still the best way to track the doings of the SF/fantasy market is to subscribe to the award-winning trade journal *Locus* (P.O. Box 13305, Oakland, CA 94661. Sample issue: $5.00).

INSTITUTIONAL

The catch-all term of "institutional" is always the crazy-quilt category of commercial and fine art, one that a paragraph can't do justice to. So I'll only briefly mention a few things that I found enjoyable. Calendars of note included those by Michael Whelan [Portal], Boris Vallejo [Workman], Alan Lee [*J.R.R. Tolkien*, Harper Collins] Simon Bisley [*Heavy Metal*], Brian Froud [*Good Faeries/Bad Faeries*, Andrews McMeel], and H.R. Giger [Morpheus], and the compilations *Monsters & Aliens* [Dark Horse] and *Martians, Mayhem & Madness* [Portal]. There were some beautiful prints and posters by Scott Gustafson, Joe DeVito, Christopher Moeller, Alex Ross, Mike Mignola, Yoshitaka Amano, and Travis Charest; tons of greeting cards; hundreds of game items; more magnets, bookmarks, and T-shirts (Graphitti Designs had some neat ones) than you can shake a stick at and much more than I could possibly list. The proverbial cup runneth over.

And isn't that great?

IN PASSING

In 1998 we said farewell to some respected members of the fantastic art community:
• Bob Kane [b. 1915], creator of Batman (with Bob Finger)
• Win Mortimer [b. 1919], comic and commercial artist
• Paul Lehr [b. 1930], SF/fine artist
• Joe Orlando [b. 1927], comic artist and Vice President at DC Comics
• Antonio Prohias [b. 1921], creator of the popular "Spy vs Spy" featured for *Mad*
• Archie Goodwin [b. 1937], comics writer, editor, and cartoonist
• Jean-Claude Forest [b. 1930], creator of the French comic strip *Barbarella*
• Alex Schomburg [b. 1905], SF/comic artist

ASFA

Although *Spectrum* no longer includes a page devoted to the Chesley Award winners, the Association of Science Fiction & Fantasy Artists is still going strong. Artists interested in joining up can write to: ASFA, P.O. Box 151311, Arlington, TX 76015-7311 USA.
                                                    †

Spectrum 6 Call For Entries Poster by Phil

artist: **JERRY LOFARO**
art director: **Dave Higgins**   *client:* **National Geographic/Lewis Galoob Toys**
title: **T-Rex Terror**   *size:* **13"x18"**   *medium:* **Acrylic**

artist: **ASHLEY WOOD**

art director: **Todd McFarlane**   *designer:* **Ashley Wood**   *client:* **Image/Todd McFarlane Entertainment**

title: **Spawn Annual**   *size:* **11"x17"**   *medium:* **Mixed/digital**

1

1
artist: BILL KOEB
designer: Bill Koeb
client: David R [CD cover]
title: Music For Mind and Feet
medium: Mixed/digital
size: 5"x5"

2
artist: BILL KOEB
art director: Allsion Burton
client: Katsin/Loeb Advertising
medium: Mixed/digital
size: 51/2"x71/2"

3
artist: GREG SPALENKA
art director: Anthony Padilla
designer: Jeff Burne
client: Art Institute of Southern California
title: Expand Your Vision
medium: Mixed/digital
size: 24"x36"

2

3

1
artist: SCOTT GRIMANDO
client: Diamond Multimedia
title: Walkabout
medium: Digital
size: 8"x10"

2
artist: DAVE DEVRIES
art director: Dana Moreshead
designer: Dave DeVries
client: Universal Studios/Marvel Entertainment
title: Fearsome 5
medium: Mixed
size: 26"x28"

3
artist: MARC SASSO
art director: Kevin Heybourne
client: Gorgon Media
medium: Oil

4
artist: R.K. POST
art director: Serge Olivier
client: Casus Belli
title: The Surgeon
medium: Oil
size: 91/2"x13"

1

2

3

4

1
artist: GARY A. LIPPINCOTT
art director: Toby Schwartz
client: Doubleday Direct
title: Story Time
medium: Watercolor
size: 18"x20"

2
artist: JERRY LOFARO
art director: Woody Litwhiler
designer: Woody Litwhiler
client: Self promotion
title: Hard Working. Gentle Disposition. Not A Bad Memory, Either.
medium: Acrylic
size: 14"x18"

3
artist: JERRY LOFARO
art director: Woody Litwhiler
designer: Woody Litwhiler
client: Self promotion
title: Industrious. Think Skinned. Perfect For Advertising.
medium: Acrylic
size: 9"x12"

4
artist: JOYCE PATTI
art director: Jim Plumeri
client: Bantam/BBC [audio tape cover]
title: The Voyage of the Dawn Treader
medium: Oil
size: 11"x18"

1

2

3

4

1
artist: DONATO GIANCOLA
art director: Ron Spears
client: Wizards of the Coast
title: Archangel
medium: Oil
size: 12"x18"

2
artist: JOHN MONTELEONE
art director: Frank Russo
designer: John Monteleone
client: Millenia Entertainment
title: Koda
medium: Oil

3
artist: GARY RUDDELL
art director: Gary Ruddell
client: Ace Books
title: Jed Is Dead
medium: Oil
size: 15"x20"

4
artist: KENT WILLIAMS
art director: Kent Williams/Brent Ashe
designer: Brent Ashe
client: Todd McFarlane Productions
title: The Crow
medium: Mixed
size: 18"x30"

1

2

3

4

artist: GARY GIANNI
art director: Marcelo Anciano   *client:* Wandering Star
title: Savage Tales of Solomon Kane   *size:* 48"x24"   *medium:* Oil

1
artist: RAY LAGO
art director: Ray Lago
designer: Greg Prusak
client: Archangel Entertainment
title: Guardian
medium: Oil
size: 9"x12"

2
artist: GRIESBACH/MARTUCCI
art director: Paolo Pépe
client: Pocket Books
title: The Messengers
medium: Oil on board
size: 24"x18"

3
artist: KINUKO Y. CRAFT
art director: Gail Dubov
designer: Gail Dubov
client: Avon Books
title: The Scent of Magic
medium: Mixed
size: 18"x24"

1

2

3

1
artist: MICHAEL DUBISCH
art director: Michael Dubisch
title: Inhumanskin: The Encounter
medium: Mixed
size: 17"x19"

2
artist: JOE JUSKO
designer: Joe Jusko
client: Byron Priess Visual Communications
title: Nick Fury
medium: Acrylic
size: 16"x26"

3
artist: ROMAS
art director: Dave Tommasino
client: Scholastic, Inc.
title: The Perils of Quadrant X
medium: Acrylic
size: 16"x24"

4
artist: ROMAS
art director: Carl Galian
client: Harper Collins
title: The Demon In the Machine
medium: Acrylic   *size:* 18"x30"

1

2

3

4

1
artist: SHAUN TAN
art director: Shaun Tan
client: Lothian Books/Melbourne
title: The Rabbits:
    "They Ate Our Grass"
medium: Acrylic & colored pencil
size: 47cmx31cm

2—4
artist: OMAR RAYYAN
art director: Regina Griffin
designer: Omar Rayyan
client: Holiday House
title: King Midas
medium: Watercolor
size: each 9¾"x10¾"

1

2

1
artist: STEPHEN YOULL
art director: Don Puckey
designer: Stephen Youll
client: Warner Books
title: Patriarch's Hope
medium: Oil
size: 28"x20"

2
artist: CHRIS MOORE
art director: Simon Weller
client: Harper Collins
title: Blindfold
medium: Acrylic
size: 21"x16"

3
artist: STEPHEN YOULL
art director: Don Puckey
designer: Stephen Youll
client: Warner Books
title: Playing God
medium: Oil

1

2

1
artist: KINUKO Y. CRAFT
art director: Jamie Warren Youll
lient: Bantam Books
title: The Silver Metal Lover
medium: Mixed
size: 18"x24"

2
artist: GARY GIANNI
art director: Marcelo Anciano
client: Wandering Star
title: Savage Tales of Solomon Kane
medium: Oil
size: 30"x40"

3
artist: MATTHEW STAWICKI
art director: Carl Gallion
client: Harper Collins
title: Fortress of Owls
medium: Digital

4
artist: GARY GIANNI
art director: Marcelo Anciano
client: Wandering Star
title: Savage Tales of Solomon Kane
medium: Oil   *size:* 30"x40"

1

2

3

4

1

2

3

1

2

3

4

1
artist: DAVE McKEAN
art director: Dave McKean/Allen Spiegel
designer: Dave McKean
client: Allen Spiegel Fine Arts/Hourglass
title: Option: Click "Wood 3"
medium: Mixed/digital
size: 9"x9"

2
artist: THOM ANG
art director: Dave Stevenson
designer: Thom Ang
client: Del Rey Books
title: Spill of Shadows
medium: Mixed/digital
size: 14"x10"

3
artist: THOM ANG
art director: Richard Thomas
designer: John Snowden
client: White Wolf
title: Angels On Fire
medium: Mixed/digital
size: 14"x10"

1

2

3

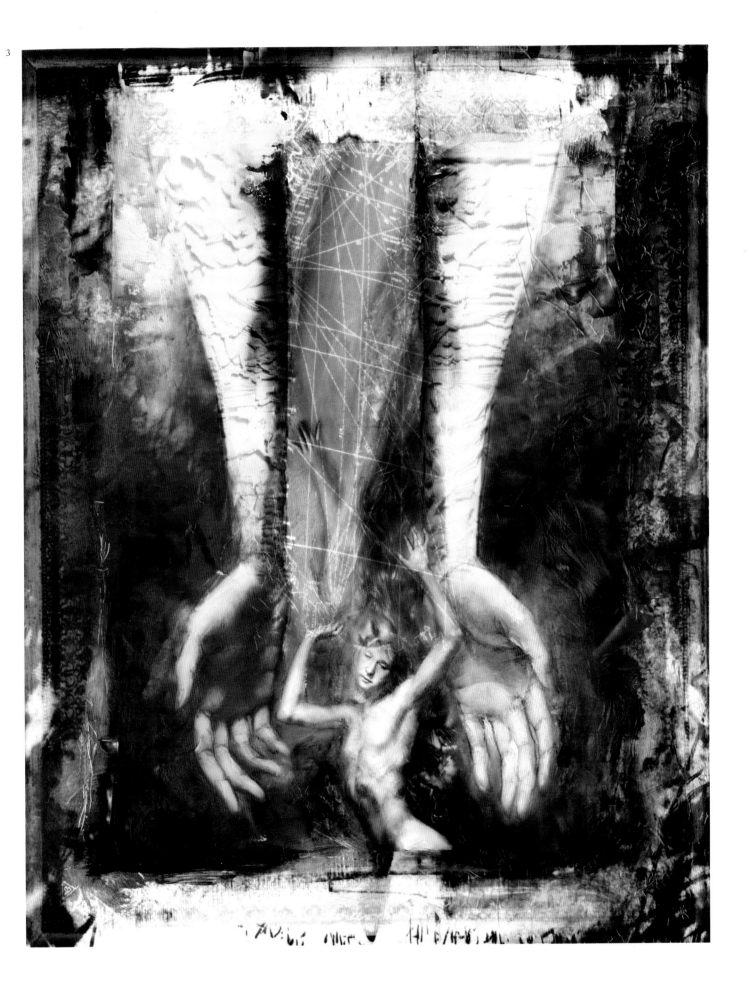

1
artist: GREG LOUDON
art director: Larry Snelly
client: White Wolf
title: Vampire: Masquerade
medium: Acrylic

2
artist: TRISTAN ELWELL
art director: Liney Li
client: Bantam Doubleday Dell
title: A Terrifying Taste
medium: Oil   *size:* 11"x16"

3
artist: CHARLES KEEGAN
art director: Jim Baen
designer: Charles Keegan/Jim Baen
client: Baen Books
title: Black As Blood
medium: Oil   *size:* 22"x30"

4
artist: ERIC PETERSON
art director: Tom Egner
client: Avon Books
title: Something Wicked
    This Way Comes
medium: Oil   *size:* 22"x24"

1

2   3

ERIC PETERSON

1
artist: YVONNE GILBERT
art director: Sheila Gilbert
designer: Miles Long
client: Daw Books
title: Wizards of the Grove
medium: Color pencils
size: 12"x18"

2
artist: DONATO GIANCOLA
client: Tor Books
title: Queen of Demons
medium: Oil
size: 34"x22"

3
artist: GORDON CRABB
art director: Sheila Gilbert
client: Daw Books
title: Spirit Fox
medium: Oil

1

2

3

1
artist: DAVE McKEAN
art director: Dave McKean/Allen Spiegel
designer: Dave McKean
client: Allen Spiegel Fine Arts/Hourglass
title: Option: Click "Rock 4"
medium: Mixed/digital
size: 9"x9"

2
artist: PHIL HALE
client: Donald Grant Books
title: Drawing of the Three
medium: Oil
size: 34"x22"

3
artist: RICK BERRY
art director: Toby Schwartz
client: Doubleday
title: The Crow
medium: Mixed/digital

4
artist: GREG SPALENKA
art director: David Stevenson
client: Random House
title: Enchantment
medium: Digital
size: 9"x12"

1

2

3

1
artist: JOHN JUDE PALENCAR
art director: David Stevenson
client: Random House/Ballantine
title: Tales of the Cthulhu Mythos
medium: Acrylic   *size:* 40"x19"

2
artist: GREG SPALENKA
title: The Witch's Dream
medium: Mixed
size: 8"x11"

3
artist: NICHOLAS JAINSCHIGG
art director: Jim Turner
designer: Lynne Condellone
client: Golden Gryphon Press
title: Eternal Lovecraft
medium: Oil   *size:* 36"x12"

1

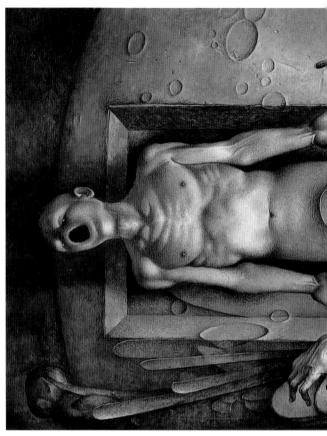

2

3

1

artist: GREG NEWBOLD
art director: Golda Laurens
client: William Morrow
title: The Lives of
        Christopher Chant
medium: Acrylic   *size:* 9"x13"

2

artist: LES EDWARDS
art director: Joy Chamberlain
client: Harper Collins
title: Fortress of Eagles
medium: Oil   *size:* 18"x24"

3

artist: BOB EGGLETON
art director: Don Puckey
client: Warner Books
title: The High House
medium: Acrylic   *size:* 28"x22"

4

artist: DON MAITZ
art director: Kevin Murphy
client: Meisha Merlin Publishing
title: Queen of Denial
medium: Acrylic
size: 13"x20"

1

2

3

4

b o o k

1
artist: JIM BURNS
art director: Richard Ogle
client: Pan Macmillan
title: The Nano Flower
medium: Digital
size: 8"x14"

2
artist: DAVE DORMAN
art director: Dave Dorman
client: Rolling Thunder
title: The Uninvited
medium: Oil & acrylic
size: 8"x14"

3
artist: JOHN HOWE
art director: Gene Mydlowski
designer: Carl Gallian
client: Harper Prism
title: Dark Heart
medium: Watercolor

4
artist: LUIS ROYO
art director: Luis Royo
client: Norma Editorial
title: Gray Over a Grayer Gray
medium: Acrylic
size: 14"x19 1/2"

1

2

3

4

1
artist: IAN MILLER
medium: Mixed

2
artist: JOHN JUDE PALENCAR
art director: Don Puckey
client: Warner Books
title: Wildseed
medium: Acrylic
size: 12"x107/8"

3
artist: DAVID BOWERS
art director: Lisa Peters
designer: Lisa Peters
client: Harcourt Brace
title: A Gathering of Gargoyles
medium: Oil on masonite
size: 111/4"x18"

1

2

3

1
artist: JOHN SULLIVAN
art director: Ridgeway Associates
client: Cassell PLC
title: World's End
medium: Oil
size: 26"x30"

2
artist: MERILEE HEYER
art director: Jennifer Brown
designer: Marilee Heyer
client: D.K. Publishing
title: Hera and Pytho
medium: Watercolor and pencil
size: 13"x15"

3
artist: CIRUELO
art director: Ciruelo
client: Wizards Publishing Group
title: Dark Stone
medium: Acrylic
size: 19"x27"

4
artist: JEAN PIERRE TARGETE
art director: Tom Egner
client: Avon Books
title: The Courts of Chaos
medium: Oil   *size:* 20"x30"

1

2

3

4

1
artist: JOHN W. SLEDD
client: Charles River Media
title: Rivety Anne
medium: Digital
size: 18"x24"

3
artist: JAMES WARHOLA
art director: Irene Gallo
client: Tor Books
title: The Callahan Chronicles
medium: Oil   *size:* 38"x18"

2
artist: CHRIS MOORE
art director: Lucie Stéricker
client: Orion Books
title: Babel 17
medium: Acrylic   *size:* 11"x16"

4
artist: JOHN ZELEZNIK
client: Palladium Books
title: Warlords of Russia
medium: Acrylic
size: 18"x24"

2

1

3

1
artist: EDWARD MILLER
art director: Alison Williams
client: Tor Books
title: The Skystone
medium: Oil

2
artist: MATILDA HARRISON
art director: Sarah Odedina
client: Bloomsbury Books
title: Bisky Bats & Pussycats
medium: Acrylic

3
artist:
JEAN PIERRE TARGETE
art director: Jamie Warren Youll
client: Bantam Books
title: The Stainless Steel Rat
medium: Oil
size: 12"x18"

4
artist: BRUCE JENSEN
art director: Irene Gallo
client: Tor Books
title: Tea From An Empty Cup
medium: Acrylic
size: 14"x20"

1

3

2

4

広島　東京

大阪

倉敷

© JENSEN 1993

artist: DAVE DeVRIES
art director: Curt Baisden   designer: Dave DeVries   client: Marvel Comics
title: The Comic Zone!   size: 13"x19"   medium: Mixed

artist: DAVE McKEAN
art director: Dave McKean   *client:* Kitchen Sink Press   *title:* Cages   *medium:* Mixed/digital

1

artist: JASON ASALA
art director: Joe Linsner
designer: Jason Asala
title: Sirius Entertainment
medium: Poe: The Haunted, Hunted Kind
medium: Mixed
size: 10"x10"

2

artist: JILL THOMPSON
art director: Joe Linsner
designer: Jill Thompson
title: Sirius Entertainment
title: Scary Godmother's Holiday Spooktacular
medium: Watercolor
size: 22"x15"

3

artist: ALEX ROSS
art director: Alex Ross
designer: Alex Ross
title: Sirius Entertainment
title: Scary Godmother
medium: Mixed
size: 11"x16"

1

2

1
artist: KEN MEYER JR
art director: Nate Pryde
designer: Ken Meyer Jr
client: Caliber Press
title: Magus
medium: Mixed/digital
size: 6"x9"

2
artist: GLEN ORBIK
art director: Joey Cavalieri
client: DC Comics
title: Legends of the DC Universe #2
medium: Oil
size: 12"x181/2"

3
artist: GLEN ORBIK
art director: Joey Cavalieri
client: DC Comics
title: Batman: Shadow of the Bat #76
medium: Oil
size: 131/2"x223/4"

4
artist: GLEN ORBIK
         & LAUREL BLECHMAN
art director: Joey Cavalieri
client: DC Comics
title: Batman: Shadow of the Bat #82
medium: Oil
size: 131/2"x223/4"

1

2

3

3

1
artist: ASHLEY WOOD
art director: Mike Marts
client: Acclaim Entertainment
title: Deadside 4
medium: Mixed/digital
size: 11"x17"

2
artist: JOSEPH MICHAEL LINSNER
art director: Joseph Michael Linsner
client: Sirius Entertainment
title: 3 Faces of Death
medium: Mixed
size: 11"x17"

3
artist: ASHLEY WOOD
art director: Mike Marts
client: Acclaim Entertainment
title: Deadside 2
medium: Mixed/digital
size: 11"x17"

4
artist: DAVE McKEAN
art director: Dave McKean
client: Kitchen Sink Press
title: Cages
medium: Mixed/digital

1

2

3

1
artist: THOMAS GIANNI
inker: Gary Gianni
client: Dark Horse Comics
title: Blowtorch Johnson
medium: Pencil, pen & ink
size: 22"x10"

2
artist: JILL THOMPSON
art director: Joe Linsner
designer: Jill Thompson
client: Sirius Entertainment
title: Scary Godmother's
         Bloody Valentine
medium: Watercolor
size: 22"x15"

3
artist: MARK CRILLEY
art director: Joe Linsner
designer: Mark Crilley
client: Sirius Entertainment
title: Akiko #26
medium: Mixed
size: 10"x14"

4
artist: DAN BRERETON
client: Dark Horse Comics
title: Punkinheads
medium: Watercolor
size: 12"x19"

5
artist: STEVE FASTNER
        & RICH LARSON
art director: Sal Quartuccio
designer: Rich Larson
client: SQP, Inc.
title: Demon Baby #3
medium: Airbrush & markers
size: 11"x17"

6
artist: VINCENT EVANS
art director: Tim Tuohy
client: Marvel Comics
title: Time Slip
medium: Oil
size: 16¾"x21¾"

All Characters ™
and Copyright © 1999 Marvel Comics.

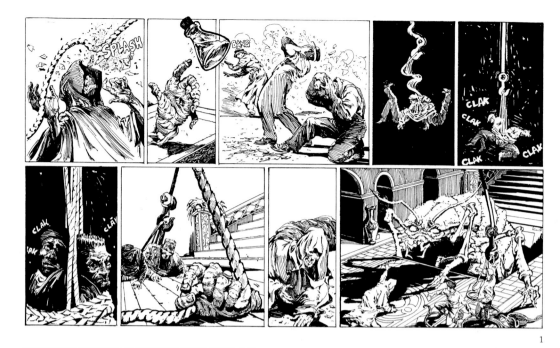

1

2

3

4

5

6

1
artist: STEVE RUDE
client: Marvel Comics/DC Comics
title: Superman vs The Hulk
medium: Oil
size: 20"x30"

The Hulk ™ and Copyright © 1999 Marvel Comics.
Superman ™ and Copyright © 1999 DC Comics.
All Rights Reserved

2
artist: CHRISTOPHER MOELLER
art director: Stuart Moore
client: DC Comics
title: Sheva's War #3
medium: Acrylic
size: 20"x30"

3
artist: CHRISTOPHER MOELLER
art director: Stuart Moore
client: DC Comics
title: Sheva's War #1
medium: Acrylic
size: 20"x30"

4
artist: RAY LAGO
art director: Madeleine Robins
designer: Joseph Caponsacco
client: Classics Illustrated/
    Acclaim Books
title: Faust
medium: Oil
size: 12 1/2"x17 1/2"

1

2

3

4

1
artist: JON J MUTH
art director: Robbin Brosterman
designer: Gearg Brewer
client: DC/Vertigo Comics
title: The Complete Moonshadow
medium: Watercolor
size: 6"x9"

2
artist: CHARLES VESS
art director: Robbin Brosterman
designer: Charles Vess
client: DC/Vertigo Comics
title: Stardust
medium: Colored inks
size: 12 1/2"x17 1/2"

3
artist: TERESE NIELSEN
art director: Dwight Jon Zimmerman
designer: Terese Nielsen
client: Topps Comics
title: Xena: The Orpheus Trilogy
medium: Acrylic/oil
size: 10 1/2"x16"

4
artist: JOSEPH MICHAEL LINSNER
art director: Joseph Michael Linsner
designer: Joseph Michael Linsner
client: Sorius Entertainment
title: Aurora Verdé
medium: Mixed
size: 12"x17"

1

2

3

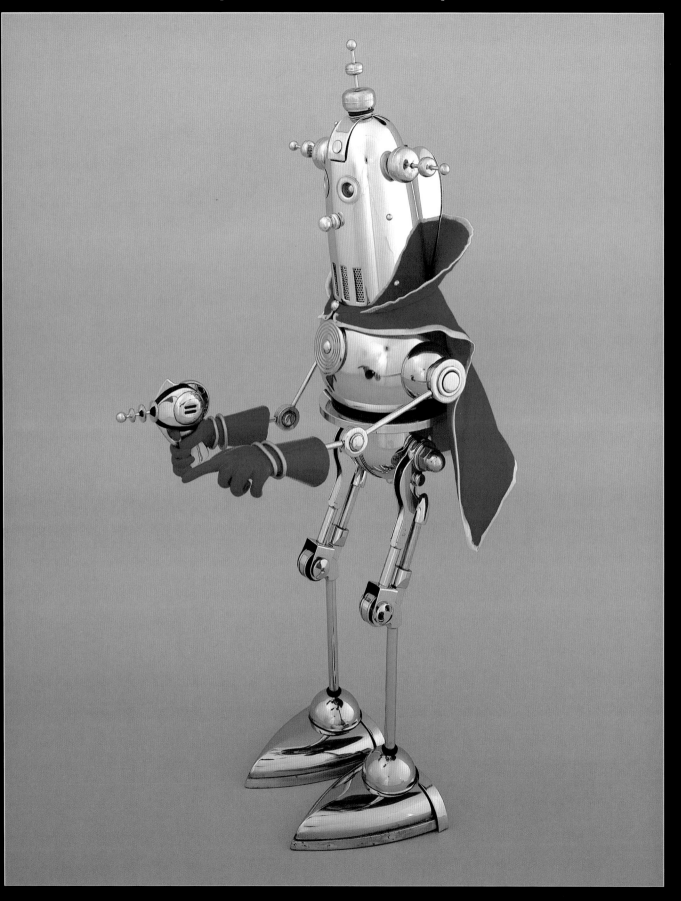

artist: LAWRENCE NORTHEY
title: Spaceman Troy   *size:* 27" tall   *medium:* Mixed

artist: **MILES TEVES**
art director: **Miles Teves**   *designer:* **Miles Teves**   *client:* **Cannom Creations**
title: **Pearl**   *size:* **13"x8"**   *medium:* **Resin**

1
artist: JAMES HAKOLA
art director: James Hakola
client: G-Zero Model Art
title: Ballistic Rose
medium: Polymer clay
size: 161/2" tall

2
artist: GRIFF JONES
designer: Griff Jones
title: Tim
medium: Paper & wire
size: 30" tall/15" wide

3
artist: HARRIETT BECKER
designer: Harriett Becker
client: Nocturnal Vision
title: The Enchantment of the Dragon Box
medium: Fired clay
size: 8" long/43/4" wide/10" tall

4
artist: TOM TAGGART
art director: Grendel
photographer: Sal Trombino
client: Jack Weinstein
title: Metatron
medium: Mixcd
size: 20"tall/16" wide

1

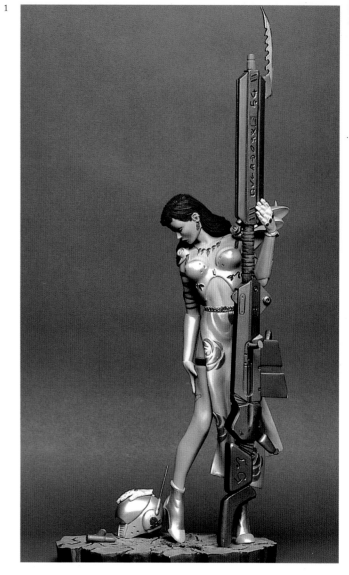

2

3

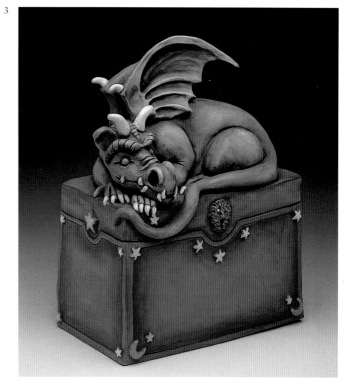

1

1
artist: RANDY BOWEN
art director: Joseph Michael Linsner
designer: Joseph Michael Linsner
client: Sirius Entertainment
title: Dawn Statue
medium: Cold-cast resin
size: 12" tall

2
artist: WILLIAM PAQUET
art director: George Brewer
designer: Steve Rude
client: DC Comics
title: Alan Scott: Green Lantern
medium: Cold-cast porcelain
size: 10 1/2" tall
Green Lantern ™ and Copyright 1999 by DC Comics. All Rights Reserved.

3
artist: MILES TEVES
designer: Miles Teves
client: Dimensional Designs
title: Swamp Witch
medium: Resin
size: 13" tall

4
artist: WILLIAM PAQUET
art director: Kim Gryzbek
designer: Glen Fabry
client: DC Comics
title: Alan Scott: Green Lantern
medium: Cold-cast porcelain
size: 10" tall
Hellblazer ™ and Copyright 1999 by DC Comics. All Rights Reserved.

2

3

1
artist: GABRIEL MARQUEZ
art director: Clayburn S. Moore
designer: Clayburn S. Moore &
        Manuel Carrasco
client: Top Cow Productions
title: Witchblade Snowglobe
medium: Cold-cast porcelain
size: 10" tall

2
artist: THE SHIFLETT BROTHERS
art director: Paul F. Moore
designer: David Mack
client: David Mack
title: Kabuki
medium: Cold-cast porcelain
size: 9 1/2" tall

3
artist: SUSUMU SUGITA
art director: Paul F. Moore & Clayburn S. Moore
designer: Marc Silvestri
client: Top Cow Productions, Inc.
title: Darkness
medium: Cold-cast porcelain
size: 14" tall

3

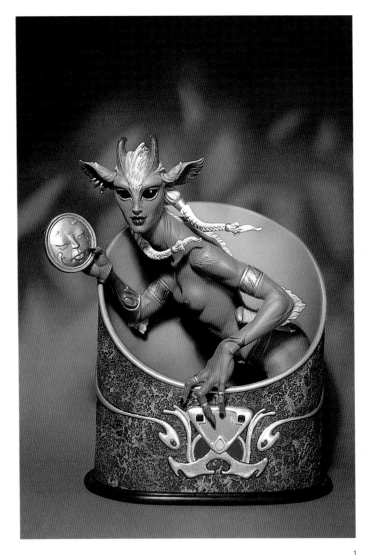

1

2

1
artist: TIM HOLTER BRUCKNER
art director: Tim Holter Bruckner
designer: Tim Holter Bruckner
client: The Art Farm
title: Diana, Goddess of the Hunt
medium: Painted resin
size: 8" tall/5 1/2" wide

2
artist: BONNIE TO
art director: Allen Spiegel
designer: John Kuramoto
client: Allen Spiegel Fine Arts
title: Princess Zula Zeleke
medium: Mixed
size: 8" tall/4" wide

3
artist: TIM HOLTER BRUCKNER
art director: Brom
designer: Brom
client: The Art Farm
title: Gazelle
medium: Painted resin
size: 14" tall/11 1/4" wide

3

1
artist: GEORGE PRATT
art director: Andrew P. Kner
designer: Andrew P. Kner
client: Scenario
title: The Fisherman
 of Beaudrais
medium: Oil
size: 18"x14"

2
artist: BROM
client: TSR
title: Priestess
medium: Oil
size: 22"x30"

3
artist: DAVE DeVRIES
art director: Jim Nelson
designer: Dave DeVries
client: FASA
title: Shadowrun
medium: Mixed
size: 10"x16"

4
artist: BROM
client: Dragon Magazine
title: The Lost Note
medium: Oil
size: 22"x30"

1

3

2

4

1
artist: PETER deSÈVE
art director: Joe Kimberling
client: Entertainment Weekly
title: Capeman Part II
medium: Watercolor
size: 10"x10"

2
artist: TONY DiTERLIZZI
designer: Larry Smith
client: Dungeon Adventures Magazine
title: The Marid Genie
medium: Watercolor/gouache
size: 15"x20"

3
artist: PETER deSÈVE
art director: Dorothy Jones
client: Dow Jones Investment Advisor
title: Trick or Treat
medium: Watercolor
size: 11"x11"

4
artist: PETER deSÈVE
art director: François Mouly
client: The New Yorker
title: In the Reading Room
medium: Watercolor
size: 10"x15"

1

2

3

1
artist: GARY KELLEY
art director: Tom Staebler
desugner: Kerig Pope
client: Playboy Magazine
title: Down In the Bahamas
medium: Pastel

2
artist: FRED FIELDS
art director: Larry Smith
client: Dragon Magazine
title: Birth of Night
medium: Oil
size: 16"x20"

3
artist: PHIL HALE
art director: Tom Staebler
desugner: Kerig Pope
client: Playboy Magazine
title: Tom Clancy's Net Force
medium: Oil
size: 34"x38"

4
artist: ZOOK
art director: Kevin Eastman
client: Heavy Metal
title: Joker's Run
medium: Oil   *size:* 16"x20"

1

2

3

e d i t o r i a l

1
artist: JILL BAUMAN
client: The Magazine of
       Fantasy & Science Fiction
title: F&SF Goes to the Movies
medium: Acyrlic
size: 14"x20"

2
artist: BARCLAY SHAW
art director: Edward L Ferman
client: The Magazine of
       Fantasy & Science Fiction
title: Backdoor Man
medium: Digital

3
artist: MARK ZUG
art director: Shauna Wolf Narciso
client: Amazing Stories
title: Recensions

4
artist: TRAVIS CHAREST
art director: Eugene Wang
designer: Eugene Wang
client: Imagine Media
title: PlayStation Magazine
medium: Mixed
size: 8"x10 1/2"

1

2

3

1
artist: PATRICK KELLEY
art director: Kinsey Caruth
client: Envoy
medium: Mixed
size: 20"x16"

2
artist: ROBERT GIUSTI
art director: Tom Staebler
designer: Kerig Pope
client: Playboy Magazine
title: Netmail

3
artist: JON VAN FLEET &
   KENT WILLIAMS
art director: Shauna Wolf Narciso
client: Amazing Stories
title: Going Native
medium: Mixed/digital

4
artist: JOHN CRAIG
art director: Shauna Wolf Narciso
client: Amazing Stories
title: It All Started By Being Amazing
medium: Mixed/collage

5
artist: RAFAL OLBINSKI
art director: Tom Staebler
designer: Len Willis
client: Playboy Magazine
title: One More Reality To Go

1

2

3

4

5

1
artist: TODD LOCKWOOD
art director: Larry Smith
client: Dragon Magazine
title: Mech Hunter
medium: Oil
size: 18"x24"

2
artist: BRYN BARNARD
art director: Bryn Barnard
client: International Studio/
    Christian Hulseman
title: Stewards of the Earth
medium: Oil
size: 48"x24"

3
artist: JANET WOOLLEY
art director: Shauna Wolf Narciso
client: Amazing Stories
title: Crane Fly
medium: Photo montage

4
artist: JANET WOOLLEY
art director: Sue Wilson
client: BBC Worldwide
title: Future Music/Tomorrow's World
medium: Photo montage

5
artist: DARREL ANDERSON
art director: Eric Courtemanche
client: Wired
title: Data Arch
medium: Digital   *size:* 17"x11"

1

2

3

4

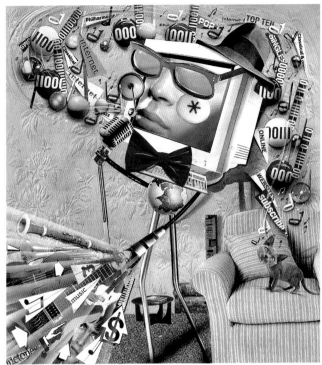

5

1
artist: ADAM HUGHES
art director: Eugene Wang
designer: Eugen Wang
client: Imagine Media
title: PlayStation Magazine
medium: Mixed
size: 8"x10½"

2
artist: MAURIZIO MANZIERI
art director: Paul Brazier
client: Interzone
title: St. Valentine's Day
medium: Digital

3
artist: D. ALEXANDER GREGORY
art director: Shauna Wolf Narciso
client: Amazing Stories
title: The Cost of Doing Business

4
artist: STEPHAN MARTINIERE
art director: Shauna Wolf Narciso
client: Amazing Stories
title: Digital Hearts and Minds
medium: Digital

1

2

3

4

artist: **ODDWORLD INHABITANTS**
art director: **Lorne Lanning**   client: **Oddworld Inhabitants**
title: **Oddworld: Abe's Exodus**   size: **7"x10"**   medium: **Digital**

1
artist: RAY-MEL CORNELIUS
client: Alternative Pick
title: Astronomy
medium: Acrylic
size: 81/2"x8"

2
artist: LARRY MacDOUGALL
art director: Patricia Lewis
client: Underhill Studio
title: Autumn Winds
medium: Watercolor
size: 9"x12"

3
artist: JAY JOHNSON
art director: Jay Johnson
client: Self promotion
title: Enchanted Dawn
medium: Digital
size: 91/4"x131/2"

1

2

3

1

1
artist: ROB JOHNSON
client: Self promotion
title: Abominable Snowman
medium: Acrylic   *size:* 12"x9"

2
artist: JON FOSTER
art director: Paul Hanchette
client: TSR
title: Raive Timogen
medium: Digital

3
artist: TRAVIS LOUIE
art director: Mark Elliott
client: Self promotion
title: Run, Pug, Run!
medium: Acrylic & ink   *size:* 30"x40"

4
artist: TODD LOCKWOOD
art director: Paul Hanchette
client: TSR
title: Spell Rune Golem
medium: Oil   *size:* 18"x24"

2

3

1
artist: KIRK REINERT
art director: Kirk Reinert
title: Night Harvest
medium: Acrylic
size: 41"x32"

2
artist: DAREN BADER
art director: Matt Wilson
client: Wizards of the Coast
title: Mirri, Cat Warrior
medium: Mixed
size: 111/2"x9"

3
artist: PETAR MESELDZIJA
client: Tjalf Sparnaay Gallery
title: The Return of
    Snow White to the
    Land of Abundance
medium: Oil
size: 191/2"x271/2"

1

2

3

1
artist: COREY MACOUREK
client: Self promotion
title: Heart
medium: Digital
size: 41/4"x6"

2
artist: MICHEL BOHBOT
art director: Michel Bohbot
designer: Michel Bohbot
client: National Labor Federation
title: Deathsquad Medicine
medium: Mixed
size: 101/2"x63/8"

3
artist: JOHN JUDE PALENCAR
art director: Toby Schwartz
client: The Science Fiction Book Club
title: The Arm of the Stone
medium: Acrylic
size: 33"x30"

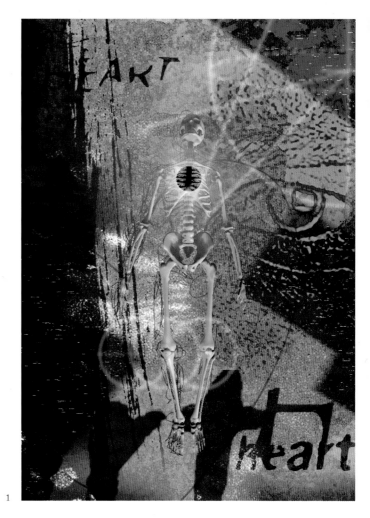

1

2

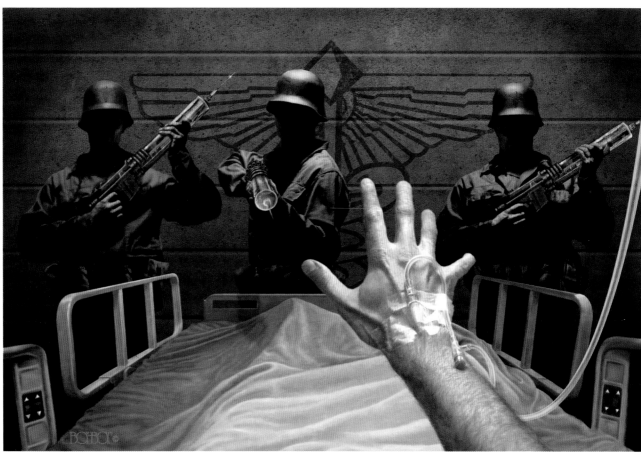

1
artist: MARC GABBANA
title: Submarine Nursery
medium: Acrylic
size: 18"x10"

2
artist: ODDWORLD INHABITANTS
art director: Lorne Lanning
client: Oddworl Inhabitants
title: Soulstorm Brewery
medium: Digital
size: 10"x61/2"

3
artist: ODDWORLD INHABITANTS
art director: Lorne Lanning
client: Oddworl Inhabitants
title: Soulstorm Mining Company
medium: Digital
size: 10"x53/8"

4
artist: MONTE MICHAEL MOORE
art director: Monte Michael Moore
client: SQP Books
title: Daydreams & Nightmares
medium: Pencil
size: 11"x17"

5
artist: EDWARD LEE
art director: Edward Lee
client: Studio Naxca
title: Extensis
medium: Digital

6
artist: TERESE NIELSEN
art director: Matt Wilson
client: Wizards of the Coast
title: Keeper of the Flame
medium: Acrylic/oil/gold leaf
size: 11"x81/2"

1

2

3

6

1
artist: ROB ALEXANDER
client: Mapleleaf Imprints
title: Sinja's World
medium: Watercolor
size: 18"x14"

2
artist: ERIC BOWMAN
client: Self promotion
title: Blue Angel
medium: Oil
size: 16"x20"

3
artist: DAVID BOWERS
title: The Fish Queen
medium: Oil
size: 9"x12"

4
artist: ASHLEY WOOD
art director: V. Jones
designer: Ashley Wood
client: Woodhaus Studios
title: Nature Mortis
medium: Mixed/digital
size: 11"x17"

1

2

3

4

1
artist: JACQUES BRÉDY
art director: Paul Hanchette
designer: Jacques Brédy
client: Wizards of the Coast
title: Alternity
medium: Oil   *size:* 18"x24"

2
artist: RON SPEARS
art director: Ron Spears
client: Deep Sea Artworks
title: Shark Gold
medium: Oil   *size:* 18"x24"

3
artist: VINCE NATALIE
client: Self promotion
title: What's Wrong With Tamara?
medium: Oil   *size:* 10"x18"

4
artist: JOSEPH DeVITO
art director: George Brewer
client: DC Comics
title: Robin
medium: Oil   *size:* 18"x28"

1

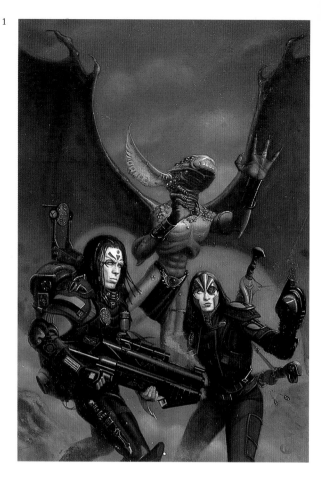

2

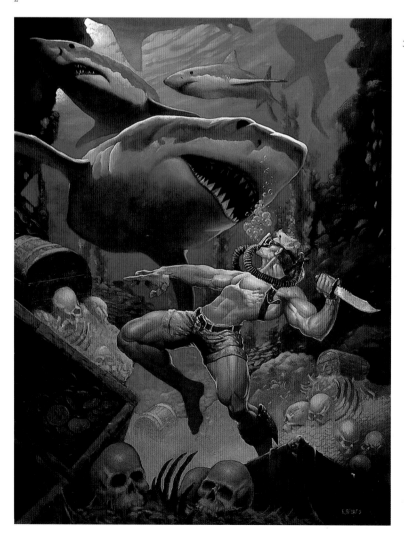

3

4

1
artist: JON FOSTER
      & RICK BERRY
medium: Digital

2
artist: GARY RUDDELL
art director: Tom Egner
client: Avon
title: Sugar Rain
medium: Oil
size: 16"x22"

1

1
artist: MICHAEL SUTFIN
title: Bringer of Torture
medium: Ink wash
size: 9"x12"

2
artist: ROBH RUPPEL
art director: Debby Jurofsky
client: Heavy Metal
title: F.A.K.K.^{2}
medium: Acrylic
size: 20"x30"

3
artist: JOE JUSKO
art director: Joe Jusko
client: Comic Images/Harris Comics
title: Vampirella
medium: Acrylic
size: 9"x12"

4
artist: MARC SASSO
art director: Jim Nelson & John Bridegroom
client: FASA
medium: Oil

2
artist: MARC GABBANA
title: Dawn of the Gargantuans
medium: Acrylic
size: 18"x10"

1

2

4

5

1
artist: KIRK REINERT
art director: Kirk Reinert
title: Celestial Friends
medium: Acrylic
size: 20"x24"

2
artist: SCOTT GUSTAFSON
art director: Scott Usher
designer: Scott Gustafson
client: The Greenwich Workshop
title: Merlin and Arthur
medium: Oil
size: 40"x24"

3
artist: DAVE DORMAN
client: Self promotion
title: Always
medium: Oil
size: 7"x10"

1

2

GOLD AWARD

[*unpublished*]

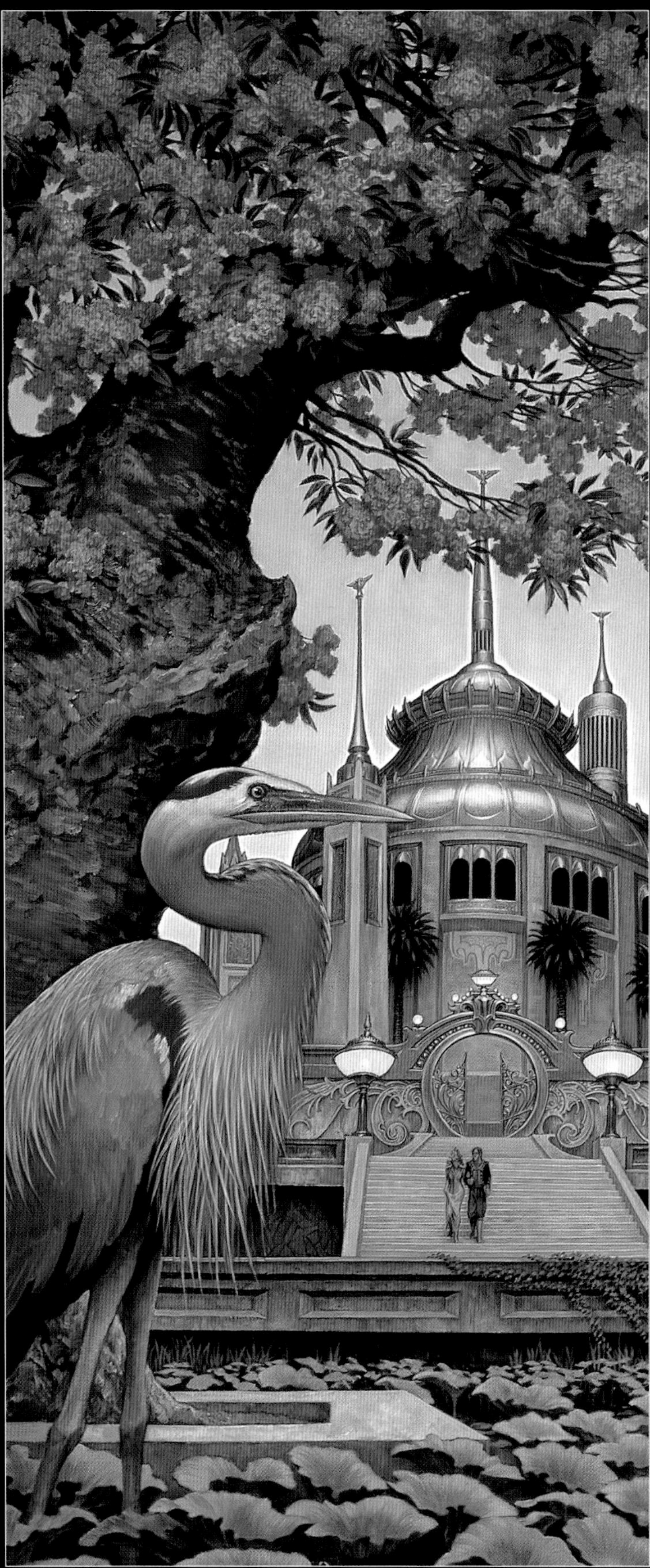

artist: **PATRICK ARRASMITH**
art director: **Patrick Arrasmith**   *title:* **Blurburn**
size: **12"x16"**   *medium:* **Scratchboard**

1

artist: ALFREDO MERCADO
medium: Oil
size: 11"x11"

2

artist: JURAJ MAXON
designer: Juraj Maxon
title: Confession of the (Poronographic)
        Funeral Petticoat
medium: Acrylic
size: 19"x24"

3

artist: PATRICK SOPER
art director: Patrick Soper
title: Oceans of an Earth-Bound Seraph
medium: Acrylic/oil
size: 24"x36"

4

artist: ALFREDO MERCADO
title: Promethean Dream
medium: Oil
size: 12"x15"

4

1
artist: DOUGLAS GRAY
title: Mermaid
size: 15" diameter

2
artist: MILES TEVES
designer: Miles Teves
title: The Temple
medium: Acrylic/oil
size: 26"x18"

3
artist: MILES TEVES
designer: Miles Teves
title: Nocturna
medium: Colored pencil
size: 81/2"x11"

1

2

3

1
artist: JASON NOBRIGA
title: Bullies
medium: Oil
size: 9"x12"

2
artist: JEFF FAERBER
medium: Mixed
size: 2'x3'

3
artist: LINO AZEVEDO
designer: Lino Azevedo
title: Natural Blindness
medium: Mixed
size: 301/2"x44"

4
artist: JASON NOBRIGA
title: Chained
medium: Oil
size: 12"x18"

1

2

3

1

1
artist: NOR
title: She
medium: Oil
size: 80"x110"

2
artist: DAVID SEELEY
title: All Mine
medium: Photo/digital

3
artist: RICK BERRY
art director: Rich Thomas
client: White Wolf
title: Ice Mother
medium: Mixed

2

1
artist: MICHAEL WHELAN
title: The End of Nature II
medium: Acrylic
size: 48"x36"

2
artist: PETER CASSELL
title: The Great Worm
medium: Acrylic
size: 12"x13"

3
artist: RICK BERRY &
    JON FOSTER
client: Neil Gaiman/
    Imagine Television
title: The Mayor
medium: Mixed

4
artist: MICHAEL WHELAN
title: Watchtower
medium: Acrylic
size: 22"x28"

1

2

3

unpublished

1
artist: ZOOK
medium: Ink
size: 18"x24"

2
artist: KYLE STILL
title: The Fiddler
medium: Acrylic
size: 24"x32"

3
artist: BLEU TURRELL
title: Siting the Enemy
medium: Acrylic
size: 13"x18½"

4
artist: KEITH PARKINSON
title: Tulak
medium: Oil
size: 8"x10"

1

2

3

1
artist: LARS GRANT-WEST
title: Lake Dragon
medium: Oil   *size:* 24"x20"

2
artist: JEFF SADOWSKI
title: Pop Goes the Dreamer
medium: Acrylic   *size:* 48"x66"

3
artist: GLEN ANGUS
title: Stormbringer
medium: Digital   *size:* 7"x9 1/2"

4
artist: LARRY REINHART
art director: Jim Salvatti
designer: Seven Reinhart
title: The Tour
medium: Mixed   *size:* 17"x11 3/4"

5
artist: LARRY REINHART
art director: Raveen Espinoza
designer: Seven Reinhart
title: Poem of the Meadows
medium: Mixed   *size:* 17"x9"

1

2

3

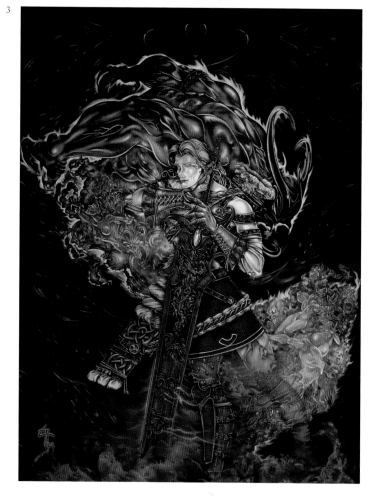

4

5

1

artist: WILLIAM STOUT
art director: Joe Rohde
designer: William Stout
client: Walt Disney Imagineering/
      Walt Disney's Animal Kingdom
title: The Kansas Sea
medium: Oil
size: 30"x18"

2

artist: JAMES GURNEY
art director: James Gurney
client: Harper Collins
title: Gideon and Avatar
medium: Oil
size: 24"x14"

3

artist: JAMES GURNEY
art director: James Gurney
client: Harper Collins
medium: Oil

4

artist: WILLIAM STOUT
designer: William Stout
client: Charles Vess/Stardust Benefit
title: Stardust Memories
medium: Ink/watercolor/colored pencils
size: 85/8"x133/4"

1

2

3

4

1
artist: CRAIG MAHER
title: Brood
medium: Oil
size: 14"x24"

2
artist: PAUL BUTVILA
title: Apparition
medium: Oil
size: 20"x30"

3
artist: LES EDWARDS
title: The Visitor II
medium: Oil

4
artist: TONY MAURO
title: Wanna Play?
medium: Digital
size: 15"x19½"

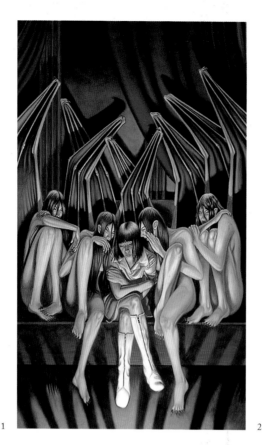

1

2

3

1
artist: MICHAEL MASCARO
client: Self promotion
title: Transformation
medium: Mixed/digital
size: 6"x6"

2
artist: RUBEN GARZA JR
client: Origin
title: Privateer—Black Star
medium: Digital
size: 17"x11"

3
artist: BILLY FALIN
title: The Obscurity Ritual
medium: Mixed/digital
size: 11"x14"

4
artist: BILLY FALIN
title: Slumbering Beauty Dreams of Fire
medium: Mixed/digital
size: 11"x14"

5
artist: MICHAEL EVANS
title: Division
medium: Digital
size: 10"x8"

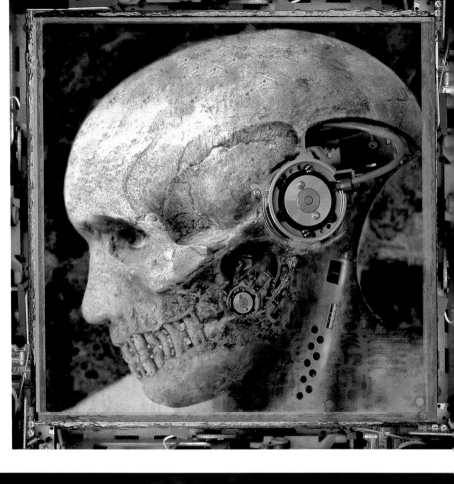

1

2

4

5

1
artist: COREY WILKINSON
title: Corporate Survival
medium: Scratchboard
size: 61/2"x9"

2
artist: JEFFREY JONES
medium: Oil

3
artist: JEFF FAERBER
title: Other Fish In the Sea
medium: Mixed
size: 12"x16"

1

2

1
artist: JEFFREY JONES
client: Michael Friedlander
title: At Rest
medium: Oil
size: 36"x32"

2
artist: RICHARD HESCOX
art director: Richard Hescox
title: The Offering
medium: Oil
size: 24"x18"

3
artist: STEPHEN HICKMAN
client: Alfred W. Roberts III
title: At the Entmoot
medium: Oil
size: 34"x34"

1

2

At the Entmoot

3

1
artist: STEPHEN HICKMAN
client: Richard & Ellen Hauser
title: Dragon
medium: Oil
size: 45"x22"

2
artist: BRAD WEINMAN
title: Nocturne
medium: Oil
size: 11"x17"

3
artist: CHRIS POLASKO
medium: Oil
size: 27"x37"

4
artist: WES BENSCOTER
title: Dragon With Devil Head
medium: Acrylic
size: 15"x18"

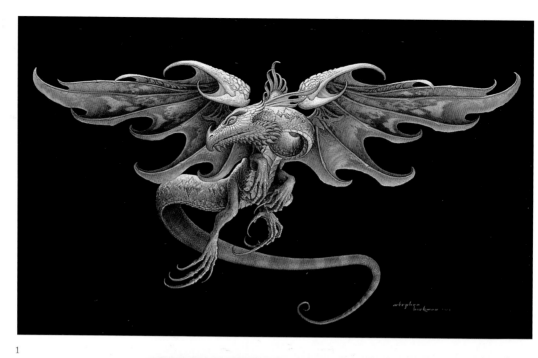

1

3

2

4

1
artist: COREY WOLFE
title: Sweet Repose
medium: Oil/acrylic
size: 30"x24"

2
artist: PAT MORRISSEY
title: Sea Monsters
medium: Oil
size: 18"x24"

3
artist: MARC FISHMAN
title: Salvation
medium: Oil
size: 36"x54"

4
artist: MARC FISHMAN
title: Perseus
medium: Oil
size: 36"x60"

1

2

3

4

1
artist: DAN BRERETON
art director: Eric Pigors
client: Toxic Toons
title: She's Just the Ghoul
    Next Door
medium: Watercolor
size: 20"x13"

2
artist: MATTHEW HAZARD
title: The Real Conspiracy
medium: Oil/acrylic
size: 10½"x13½"

3
artist: CHRIS HAWKES
title: Ex-1
medium: Mixed
size: 7½"x10"

4
artist: DAN BRERETON
art director: Eric Pigors
client: Toxic Toons
title: Haunted Garden
medium: Watercolor
size: 13"x20"

1

2

3

4

1
artist: HUGO WESTPHAL
medium: Oil

2
artist: ANDREW GOLDHAWK
title: Crash Landing
medium: Oil
size: 18"x24"

3
artist: JAMES BROOKS TOST
title: Lord Reaver
medium: Mixed
size: 11"x17"

4
artist: MARK A. NELSON
art director: Mark A. Nelson
client: Grazing Dinosaur Press
title: Fertility: E2
medium: Colored pencil
size: 10"x15"

1

2

3

1
artist: PATRICK ARRASMITH
title: Apsara
medium: Scraperboard
size: 10"x17"

2
artist: MICHAEL D. PAGE
medium: Oil
size: 11"x15"

3
artist: DOMINICK SAPONARO
medium: Oil
size: 18"x28"

4
artist: BRIGID MARLIN
title: The Rod
medium: Oil/egg tempera
size: 48"x36"

1

2

3

4

1
artist: JOSEPH KRESOJA
client: Nectar Studios
title: Birth
medium: Oil
size: 42"x42"

2
artist: THOMAS M. BAXA
title: Burning Head Ritual
medium: Oil
size: 18"x24"

3
artist: FRANK DIXON
title: Little Tree's Fear
medium: Mixed
size: 15"x20"

4
artist: ANITA SMITH
title: Sleep Till Dusk
medium: Oil
size: 24"x30"

1

2

3

4

1
artist: JAMES CANIGLIA
title: Brain Storm
medium: Mixed
size: 20"x20"

2
artist: WILLIAM O'CONNOR
title: Mechopolis
medium: Oil
size: 36"x24"

3
artist: KEN MEYER JR
client: Scott Sewell
title: Satiated
medium: Watercolor
size: 15"x20"

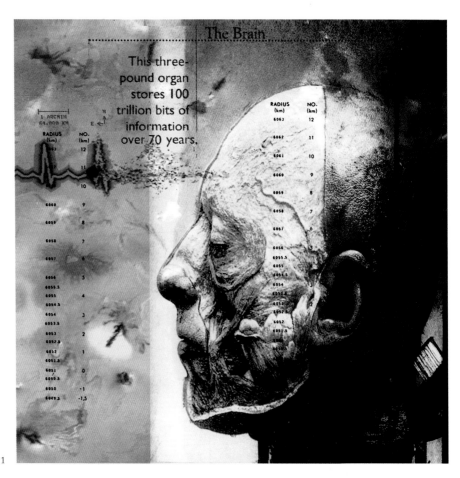

1

2

1
artist: FRANK CHO
title: Princess Revenge
medium: Pen & ink
size: 11"x17"

2
artist: SCOTT M. FISCHER
title: B.A.M.F.
medium: Oil

3
artist: DAVE DOUGLAS
title: Brynhild
medium: Mixed
size: 25"x35"

4
artist: ANDY CHUNG

2

3

4

1
artist: RICHARD LAURENT
client: Laurent Design
title: Jacob's Ladder
medium: Pen & ink
size: 12"x12"

2
artist: MARK HARRISON
title: Draco Niger Grandis
medium: Acrylic
size: 28"x18"

3
artist: DAVE DEVRIES &
      TOM TAGGART
client: Four Color Images Gallery
title: Ed Lemco's Day At the Beach
medium: Mixed
size: 30"x35"

1

2

3

1
artist: DON MAITZ
client: Howard Frank
title: King Solomon's Mines
medium: Oil
size: 40"x30"

2
artist: WILLIAM STOUT
medium: Oil

3
artist: ALAN POLLACK
client: Pinnacle Entertainment
title: Jacko
medium: Oil
size: 18"x24"

4
artist: ERIC BOWMAN
title: Egyptian Fly Girl
medium: Acrylic
size: 11"x14"

1

2

3

4

1
artist:
MARYLYN MODNY

2
artist:
DARREL ANDERSON
title: Pipeorgan
medium: Digital

3
artist:
JOHN JUDE PALENCAR
title: Storm Worship
medium: Acrylic
size: 34"x30"

4
artist: PHIL HALE
title: Can I Change My Mind
If I Want To?
medium: Oil
size: 40"x62"

2

1

3

4

Rob Alexander 116
PO Box 178
Vida, OR 97488
541-896-0283
em: robalex@teleport.com

Darrel Anderson 101, 172
1585 Territory Trail
Colorado Springs, CO 80919
719-535-0407
http://www.braid.com

Thom Ang 42, 43
c/o Allen Spiegel Fine Arts
221 Lobos Ave.
Pacific Grove, CA 93950
408-372-4672

Glen Angus 140
1420 Blairwood Crs
Windsor, Ontario
Canada N8W 5M6
519-972-5942

Patrick Arrasmith 127, 160
309 6th St./#3
Brooklyn, NY 11215
718-499-4101

Jason Asala 66
c/o Sirius Entertainment
264 E Blackwell St
Dover, NJ 07801
973-328-1455

Lino Azevedo 132
834 Jackson St.
Santa Clara, CA 95050
408-244-8303
www.thegrid.net/insaneimage

Darin Bader 110
625 Poinsettia Park N
Encinitas, CA 92024
760-632-1618

Byrn Barnard 100
432 Point Caution Dr.
Friday Harbor, WA 98250
360-378-6355

Jill Bauman 96
67-24 Utopia Parkway
Fresh Meadows, NY 11365
718-886-5616

Thomas Baxa 162
5051 Alton Parkway #192
Irvine, CA 92604

Wes Benscoter 153
5532 Ridgeview Dr
Harrisburg, PA 17112
717-545-7221 [fax]
www.wesbenscoter.com

Rick Berry 48, 120, 135, 136
93 Warren St.
Arlington, MA 02174
http://www.braid.com

Laurel Blechman 69
818-785-7904

Michel Bohbot 112
3823 Harrison St.
Oakland, CA 94611
510-547-0667

Randy Bowen 82

David Bowers 57, 116
206 Arrowhead Ln.
Eighty-Four, PA 15330
724-942-3274
724-942-3276[fax]

Eric Bowman 104, 116, 171
7405 SW 154th Place
Beaverton, OR 97007
503-644-1016

Jacques Bredy 118
c/o Terri Shirley-Summerhayes
101 E RT 70/ #169
Marlton, NJ 08053
609-985-0854

Daniel Brereton 73, 156, 157
P.O. Box 9177
Truckee, CA 96162
em: dbrereton@compuserve.com

Brom
2916- 90, 91218th Ave. SE
Issaquah, WA 98029
em: morb@jps.net

Tim Holter Bruckner 86, 87
256 125th St.
Amery, WI 54001
715-268-7291
715-268-4139 [fax]

Jim Burns 54
c/o Alan Lynch
11 King's Ridge Rd.
Long Valley, NJ 07853
908-813-8718

Paul Butvila 144
1545 Renfrew St.
Vancouver, BC
Canada V5K 4C8

Ciruelo Cabral 58
PO Box 57
08870 Sitges
Barcelona, Spain
34-938946761 [fax]
ciruelo@dac-editons.com

Jeremy E. Caniglia 164
1323 Jackson St. #214
Omaha, NE 68106
402-341-3194
www.caniglia-art.com

Peter Cassell 136
517 Hazel Ave.
San Bruno, CA 94066

Travis Charest 97
c/o Eugene Wang
150 N Hill Dr / #40
Brisbane, CA 94005

Frank Cho 166
7844 Saint Thomas Dr.
Baltimore, MD 21236
410-661-6897

Andy Chung 167
1828 Paseo Azul SE
Rowland Hts, CA 91748
626-913-4138

Ray-Mel Cornelius 106
1526 Elmwood Blvd.
Dallas, TX 75224
214-946-9405
214-946-5209 [fax]

Gordon Crabb 47
c/o Alan Lynch
11 King's Ridge Rd.
Long Valley, NJ 07853
908-813-8718

Kinuko Y. Craft 29, 36
83 Litchfield Rd.
Norwalk, CT 06058
860-542-5018

John Craig 99

Mark Crilley 73
c/o Sirius Entertainment
264 E Blackwell St
Dover, NJ 07801
973-328-1455

Peter deSève 92, 93
25 Park Place
Brooklyn NY 11217
718-398-8099

Joseph DeVito 119, 176
11 Shady Hill Dr.
Chalfont, PA 18914
215-822-3002

David DeVries 20, 64, 90, 169
67 Benson Dr.
Wayne, NJ 07470
973-696-3782
em: turbobonn@aol.com

Tony Diterlizzi 92
190 Garfield Place #4B
Brooklyn, NY 11215
718-768-8044

Frank Dixon 162
723 East Ave. #J-9
Lancaster, CA 93535
661-940-9839

Dave Dorman 54, 125
P.O. Box 15.
Shalimar, FL 32579
em: webmaster@dormanart.com

Dave Douglass 167
6251 Ridgebury Blvd.
Cleveland, OH 44124
440-442-3283

Michael Dubisch 30
15 Sieber Rd.
Kerhonkson, NY 12446
914-626-4386
em: fanvisions@aol.com

Les Edwards 52, 144
c/o Alan Lynch
11 Kings Ridge Rd.
Long Valley, NJ 07853
908-813-8718
908-813-0076[fax]

Bob Eggleton 52
P.O. Box 5692
Providence, RI 02903
em: zillabob@ids.net

Tristan Elwell 44
41 Main St.
Dobbs Ferry, NY 10522
914-674-9235

Michael Evans 147
15 B Stillwell St.
Matawan, NJ 07747
732-290-7458

Vincent Evans 73
331 E 116th St
New York, NY 10029

Jeff Faerber 132, 149
1423 Gaucho Ct.
San Jose, CA 95118
408-265-2329
em: jfaerber@hotmail.com

Billy Falin 147
281 Fairgrounds Rd.
Painesville, OH 44077
em: billyfalin@aol.com

Steve Fastner & Rich Larson 73
529 S 7th St. #445
Minneapolis, MN 55415
612-338-0959

Fred Fields 94
7536 Carole Ln.
Florence, KY 41042

Scott M Fischer 167
846 Rt 203
Spencertown, NY 12165
518-392-7034
em: greenfish@aol.com

Marc Fishman 154, 155
14440 Dickens St. #305
Sherman Oaks, CA 91423
212-802-9821

Jon Foster 108, 120, 136
231 Nayatt Rd.
Barrington, RI 02806
401-245-8438

Marc Gabbana 114, 123
2453 Olive Rd.
Windsor, ONT
Canada N8T 3N4
519-948-2418

Ruben Garza Jr. 146
4600 Seton Center Parkway #827
Austin, TX 78759
512-794-0222

Donato Giancola 24, 40, 41, 46, 89
397 Pacific St
Brooklyn, NY 11217
718-797-2438
718-797-4308 [fax]

Gary Gianni 27, 36, 37
2540 W Pensacola
Chicago, IL 60618

Thomas Gianni 72
5521 W. Grace
Chicago, IL 60641

Yvonne Gilbert 46
c/o Alan Lynch
11 King's Ridge Rd.
Long Valley, NJ 07853
908-813-8718

Robert Giusti 98

Andrew Goldhawk 158
5125 Williams Fork Tr. #203
Boulder, CO 80301
303-516-1865

Douglas Gray 130
54 Esplanade Rd.
Scarborough•N•Yorks
England 7011 2AU
+44 (0) 1723 360312

Scott Grimando 20
6-Fifth Ave.
Westbury, NY 11590
http://home.earthlink.net/~stgrimm

D. Alexander Gregory 102

James Gurney 142
P.O. Box 693
Rhinebeck, NY 12572

Scott Gustafson 124
4045 N. Kostner Ave
Chicago, IL 60641
773-725-8338
773-725-5437[fax]

James Hakola 80
P.O. Box 171
Los Alamitos, CA 90720

Phil Hale 48, 94, 173
25A Vyner St.
London, UK E29DG

John Harris
c/o Alan Lynch
11 King's Ridge Rd.
Long Valley, NJ 07853
908-813-8718

Mark Harrison 168
Flat 3/13 Palmeira Ave.
Hove E. Sussex, UK BN3 3GA
01273 739 286

Matilda Harrison 62
c/o Alan Lynch
11 King's Ridge Rd.
Long Valley, NJ 07853
908-813-8718

Chris Hawkes 156
785 W 1400 S
Woods Cross, UT 84087
801-294-5518

Matthew Hazard 156
717 Rowland Blvd.
Novato, CA 94947
415-893-9885
em: vpaint@sirius.com

Richard Hescox 150
28015 SE 221st St.
Maple Valley, WA 98038
richh@premier1.net

Marilee Heyer 58
1619 6th St.
Los Osos, CA 93402

Stephen Hickman 126, 151, 152
10 Elm Street
Red Hook, NY 12571

John Howe 54
c/o Alan Lynch Rep.
11 King's Ridge Rd.
Long Valley, NJ 07853
908-813-8718

Adam Hughes 102
c/o Eugene Wang
150 N Hill Dr / #40
Brisbane, CA 94005

Nicholas Jainschigg 50
80 King St
Warren, RI 02885
401-245-2954
401-245-5145 [fax]

Bruce Jensen 63
3939 47th St.
Sunnyside, NY 11104
718-482-9125

Jay Johnson 107
333 Melrose Dr. #3D
Richardson, TX 75080
972-231-7448
972-675-1841 [fax]

Rob Johnson 108
c/o Donna Rosen Rep.
15209 Rockport Dr
Silver Spring, MD 20905
301-384-8925

Griff Jones 80
8505 E Hampden Ave. #13P
Denver, CO 80231

Jeffrey Jones 148, 150

Joe Jusko 30, 123
35 Highland Rd/ #4404
Pittsburgh, PA 15102
412-833-7528

Charles Keegan 44
P.O. Box 2532
Forest Park, GA 30297
404-366-1490
404-366-2762 [fax]

Gary Kelley 88, 94

Patrick Kelley 98
1040 Veto St.
Grand Rapids, MI 49504
616-458-5925

Bill Koeb 18
1234 4th Ave.
San Francisco, CA 94122
415-665-1913
em: billkoeb@koeb.com

Joseph Kresoja
1243 5th Ave. 162N #4
Seattle, WA 98109
206-285-4858

Ray Lago 28, 74
P.O. Box 36
Jersey City, NJ 07303
201-653-0241

Richard Laurent 168
531 S Plymouth Ct.
Chicago, IL 60605
312-939-7130
312-939-1875 [fax]

Edward Lee 115
351 S Fuller Ave. #6C
Los Angeles, CA 90036
323-857-1134

Joseph Michael Linsner 70, 77
c/o Sirius Entertainment
264 E Blackwell St
Dover, NJ 07801
973-328-1455

Gary A. Lippincott 22
131 Greenville Rd.
Spencer, MA 01562
508-885-9592
www.garylippincott.com

Todd Lockwood 100, 109
20523 125th St. CT E
Bonney Lake, WA 98390
253-826-2265

Jerry LoFaro 16, 22
58 Gulf Rd
Henniker, NH 03242
603-428-6135
603-428-6136 [fax]

Greg Loudon 44
1804 Pine Rd.
Homewood, IL 60430
708-799-4339
708-798-5936 [fax]

PAINTING BY JOSEPH DeVITO

The titles and body copy of this book was set in the Adobe version of the Caslon.
Spectrum 6 was designed on both a Macintosh G3 and a 7200Power PC.

Book design and typography by *Arnie Fenner.*
Art direction and editing by *Cathy Fenner* and *Arnie Fenner.*

Printed in Hong Kong.

ARTISTS, ART DIRECTORS AND PUBLISHERS INTERESTED IN RECEIVING
ENTRY INFORMATION FOR THE NEXT SPECTRUM COMPETITION
should send their name and address to:

Spectrum Design
P.O. Box 4422
Overland Park, KS
66204-0422

Call For Entries posters are mailed out in Sept./Oct. each year.